China Boat Boy

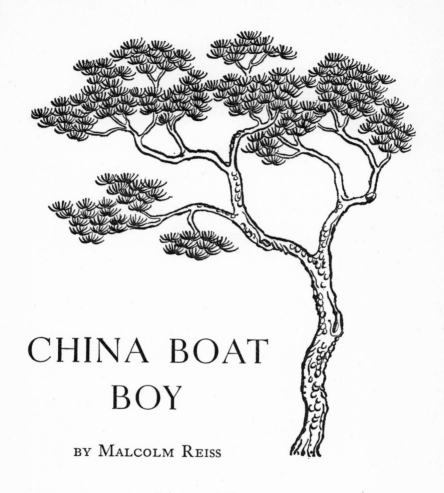

CHINA BOAT BOY

BY MALCOLM REISS

ILLUSTRATED BY JEANYEE WONG

J. B. LIPPINCOTT COMPANY   PHILADELPHIA
NEW YORK

CONTENTS

One   THE SILVER BIRD 11

Two   THE LOLO KNIFEMEN 19

Three   SHIPWRECK 29

Four   STRANGE REFUGE 35

Five   SCARFACE TAKES HIS REWARD . . . 40

Six   A LONG ARM REACHES 50

Seven   HOW FENG CAME TO CLAIM PRECIOUS
GRIEF 59

Eight   ON THE CHENGTU ROAD 67

Nine   FENG'S HIRED ASSASSIN 73

Ten   THE RIM OF TIBET 83

Eleven   "THE LONGEST JOURNEY STARTS WITH
A SINGLE STEP". 91

Twelve   THE IMPERIAL BEGGAR 96

Thirteen   S O S FOR CAPTAIN SCOTT 104

Fourteen   LONG WAITING 111

Fifteen   A TRAP FOR THE UNWARY 124

Sixteen   THE RAID 130

Seventeen   DISAPPEARANCE 137

Eighteen   THE GILDED COFFIN 143

Nineteen   SCARFACE SAYS GOOD-BYE 149

Twenty   THE BRIDGE OF CHIN PI LU 153

ILLUSTRATIONS

Tien tai-tai had never dictated a letter before . . . 23

"You are the family Tien?" 51

Sui was still waving his arms 81

Joe shot off down the road 113

Something streaked by Chuck's ear 141

China Boat Boy

Chapter One

THE SILVER BIRD

T HE moon and the sun are the symbols of Kunming. The Tien family and the redheaded American flyer were as far apart as the sun and the moon but they met, there on the edge of the red-walled city, and for a bit their lives ran parallel.

It started the day that Precious Grief got away. Usually the fishing bird seldom left the sampan except upon Chuck's shoulder but the noise and bustle of the lake-harbor must have drawn the cormorant for suddenly little Pung noticed that their pet was gone.

"Precious Grief!" he shouted. "Precious Grief!"

Chuck, and Tien tai-tai, their mother, bounced from the cabin, looking about wildly. Beyond a pile of raw teak Chuck thought he saw a wing flash. He leapt ashore. Pung followed on stubby legs.

They spotted Precious Grief on the far side of the lumber pile, head cocked with mischief. With a shout the two boys scuttled after him. Fortunately cormorants are awkward flyers and poor runners. Still, Precious Grief led the boys a merry chase.

"Get him. Get him," yelped Pung.

Precious Grief waddled between rickshaws and carts, in and out among the sunflower-seed booths. Men shouted cheap advice as Chuck and Pung raced after their cormorant. Finally the boys cornered him. Precious Grief was heaving from his unusual exertions.

"You water-crow, you," said Chuck, grabbing the bird roughly. "I should paddle your bare soles for this."

Pung offered a couple of threats of his own.

As they walked back along the quay the boys suddenly ran into an unusual sight—an American in sheepskin-lined jacket and fifty-mission cap was arguing with some boatmen.

Only a few years before, when Chennault's Flying Tigers had been headquartered in Kunming, Americans were all over the place. Flyers and ground troops had long since gone back over the Hump, leaving nothing but the memory of their laughter and their rough and breezy ways. But this American would have caught the boys' attention at any time. He was huge, as tall as the Lohan that guard the Temple of the Western Cloud. Under his cap the American's hair was the red of temple-cloth and his face more or less matched his hair. His jaunty flight jacket carried the CNAC patch.

"You fellows are nothin' but bandits," he was telling the boatmen in Mandarin mixed with hunks of Texas. "Where are your guns, you slant-eyed Jesse Jameses?"

The boatmen shook their fists, trading insult for insult.

"Great day in the morning!" growled the flyer. "Let's have a fair price or I'll find another outfit to ferry my stuff."

"No, no, no. Good price. *Ding hao* price," shrieked the boatmen in pidgin English.

The American let out a grunt and turned away.

Chuck and Pung followed. When they were out of sight of the other boatmen, Chuck called out, "Wait, please, wait."

The tall flyer turned. "What do you want?" he asked in his queerly accented Mandarin.

"We have a sampan," said Chuck quickly. "We could ferry the tile."

Slowly a grin replaced the flyer's anger. "All right. Let's have a look at your barge."

Chuck's mother welcomed the stranger with her friendly smile, the smile she could give as easily to beggars as to mandarins. The American looked over the sampan with a cargo-pilot's eye. "Kind of puny," he said, "but you should be able to ferry the stuff in maybe twenty-five or thirty trips."

Over a cup of tea they closed the deal. Captain Scott told the Tiens that he was with China National Airways and that the tile was for a new hostel to be built on the outskirts of Kunming. They had trouble following the American's speech at times for he spoke the Mandarin dialect with a Texas twang, and even some English words thrown in. But that didn't matter, the Tiens were happy. It meant a month's work at good pay. It meant food. Tien tai-tai and the boys had often been hungry since the boys' father had been taken away.

As the American climbed out of the sampan, Chuck and Pung leapt ashore. The man grinned down at the two boys.

"You've got savvy, kids. Maybe some day instead of this

old bumboat of yours you'll have a squadron of Douglases flitting back and forth across the Hump."

Chuck and Pung didn't quite understand for the American was mixing his Chinese and English as usual, but at least they got the gist.

"Okay," Chuck grinned, using his one American word. Pung echoed him, "O-kay."

The flyer flung a wide salute and was off down the quay.

After the American had left there was much excitement. Tien tai-tai hugged Chuck and Pung. She laughed and cried. Since he had been the cause of leading the boys to the wonderful, if slightly mad American, Precious Grief was fed an extra fistful of bean curd. But he was still annoyed at being chased, and in between beakfuls he stood on one leg and clacked.

Precious Grief had always been an odd and mischievous character. At night he slept between the boys, making himself as large as an official's wife. He rode on Chuck's or Pung's shoulder when they poled the sampan. As well as diving for fish he was fond of going after bright stones or bits of glass, anything the boys tossed overboard.

He was greedy, too. Rusty nails, fishbones, scraps of cloth—Precious Grief gobbled anything that attracted his eye.

Tien, his master, used to shake his head and laugh. "That bird must have the insides of a gristmill."

Many cormorants are bright and affectionate and almost all of them are greedy but Precious Grief was unusual in still another respect. He was not cormorant color which is black or dirty brown. Precious Grief was the color of rain lit by sunlight. His coat was a glowing silver. None of the fishermen on Lake Tien Chih had ever seen a cormorant like Precious Grief. Only Tien, who had owned the bird since Chuck was a small boy, knew where the silver cormorant came from. It was an odd story. Tien had told no one. He had promised the beggar that he would say nothing and Tien was one to keep his promises.

The windy night that the beggar came, Tien had been alone. The man was dressed in rags. His feet were bleeding. He came to the sampan about midnight and quietly awakened Tien. "Boatman," he said fiercely, "I must cross the lake. I'm in a hurry."

He must have noticed that Tien was staring at him oddly for he said, "I'll pay you well, don't worry." He took out ten *taels* of silver from his rags and laid them neatly on the mat in the bottom of the sampan. Then Tien knew for certain that here was no beggar though he'd guessed as much from the way the man spoke.

They sailed west across the lake towards the mountains. Here began many mountain paths leading to the China border, to the passes of the Himalayas, and on to Burma beyond. By a point of land where the woods came down protectively to the lake's edge, Tien lowered his sail. He put out a plank so that the man could step ashore without getting wet.

"Courtesy from a boatman!" the beggar said bitterly. "Well I have a gift for you, boatman. Not exactly a gift. Rather something to guard for the sake of China."

From his pack he drew a cage decorated with lapis lazuli morning-glories. The tiny cage held a young cormorant in a nest of cotton. However the bird was like no cormorant fledgling that Tien had ever seen. It was white—milk white, moonstone white—and beautiful.

The beggar said, "Feed him carefully. *Toy-fu* and finely minced raw meat. And once in a while mix some pepper in his food. He's the last of the Imperial breed, the last of the Rain Birds. As long as the breed goes on, so the scholars have always claimed, there will be greatness for China."

Then the beggar left quickly. But as he was slinging on his pack he said to Tien, "Once I was rich and proud. Too proud, perhaps. Now I have little left but the pack on my back and this silver fledgling. I give you the cormorant because the bird doesn't really belong to me—it belongs to China. Tell no one that you've seen me. And don't tell anyone where you got the bird. Promise me, boatman?"

Tien promised.

That was the last he ever saw of the man. In fact it was the last he ever heard of him until much later, up in Chengtu near Tibet, when a priest told him that he, too, had seen the beggar.

Precious Grief came by his name oddly, too. Originally the bird had been called Precious One because of his rare coloring and proud bearing. Then one day when Precious One had pecked little Pung—pecked him so hard that Pung had taken a header into the lake—Tien tai-tai had said angrily, "Some day that bird will bring us all to grief." From then on the boys had called their pet Precious Grief.

In the years that followed, misfortune had often found the Tien family—as it might any family in China. First Tien himself had been seized by an army press gang and hustled off to fight in one of China's endless wars.

That same summer the monsoon rains had never stopped. The countryside was flooded. Mud from the hills poured into Lake Tien Chih so that for months there was no fishing. In desperation Tien tai-tai had pawned Tien's cormorants with an old man known as Feng of the Buzzards. People said that Feng knew more about birds and more about evil than any man in China. Precious Grief, too, was pledged to Feng. Misfortune had certainly taken a fancy to the Tiens. But never, even in their darkest moments, did they blame Precious Grief.

Even misfortune can't run endlessly. With the advent of the redheaded American a change seemed to have come into the Tiens' life. They were ferrying their second load of tile up the lake towards Kunming, running sluggishly before the wind, when Pung noticed a craft bearing down upon them.

"Look, look," he cried, recognizing a friend. He might have fallen overboard as he was fond of doing if Tien tai-tai had not gripped him by the slack of his pants.

It was old Wu, the fisherman.

"Ei-yi," he complained as he pulled alongside. "For three weeks I've been hunting you. I've got a letter from Tien."

Tien tai-tai's voice sang. "Quickly, give it to me."

With her faded pantaloons puffed by the gay lake breeze she leapt to Wu's boat. Holding the letter against her heart she leapt back to her sampan.

"May it be good news," Wu called cheerily.

Tien tai-tai waved, happy as a girl.

"Steer for Chengkong," she told Chuck. She opened the letter and sat looking at it even though she couldn't read a single character.

They headed east. Loaded down with spinach-green roof tile, the fishing sampan made slow time. As he swung the oar Chuck thought, if I ever get a chance I'll learn to read.

Now it was like hearing his father's voice without being able to catch a single word.

As he rowed Chuck thought of the last time he had seen Tien.

Chapter Two

THE LOLO KNIFEMEN

IT was during the New Year's celebration. He and Tien tai-tai and Pung had walked into the city to see the dragon dance and watch the celebration. They had bought a square of blue cloth to patch Pung's pants and some hanks of red thread and a twistful of sesame. They were returning to their sampan, which lay in the river, laughing about the sights they had seen, when Tien tai-tai noticed the crowd at Chin Pi Lu Bridge. Tien tai-tai had stopped in her tracks.

It was a curious, angry crowd. Chuck saw his father, usually tall and jaunty, being buffeted about. Tien looked jaunty no longer, he looked uncertain and scared. Soldiers reared out of the crowd, swinging their brass-buckled belts, slashing a path for themselves and their prisoners.

A boatman shouted, "You can't take the fisherman. He's got a family."

The sergeant whacked the man across the face. "He's got a family, has he," he mimicked. "Out of my way, river rat, or I'll grab you too."

Tien tai-tai was weeping and beating her way through the crowd with her market basket. Tien saw her, and called above the growl of the mob, "It's no use."

Chuck saw then that his arms were tied. The rope led to two other men who were similarly tied.

"I'll come back," Tien shouted as the soldiers hustled him along the cobbled road leading east from Kunming. "I'll come back. I'll meet you here at Chin Pi Lu Bridge. . . ." He saw Chuck and Pung in the thinning crowd. "Good-bye, Pung." And to Chuck he called, "Take care of the family, Eldest Son."

Then the soldiers marched him away.

Chuck sighed. He often thought of the day they had taken Tien. But his father must be alive if he had sent a letter.

Pung was babbling as usual. Chuck put aside his own thoughts for a moment to listen to what Pung was saying.

"Our luck day. Our luck day. Our luck day," Pung was saying over and over again.

Chuck grinned. Perhaps Pung was right. Chuck put his weight into the forward thrust of the oar.

The elder was sitting in his courtyard contemplating his camellia trees, not yet in bloom but beautiful in the feel of their twisted branches. When the old man saw what the Tiens wanted he smiled. How much a word meant to the young, how little it meant to the old! Out of a sharkskin case the elder drew his square glasses. Tien tai-tai and her sons squatted on the flagstones of the courtyard that was silent except for the icy tinkle of crystal wind chimes.

"Your husband is in good health. He is with a Yunnanese regiment. He has friends and they often speak of Lake Tien Chih. He hopes you are managing without him. He sends his highest affection to you, Tien tai-tai, and to his boys. He hopes that the fishing has been good."

The old scholar stopped and lifted the mulberry sheet closer to his eyes. "It says," he added, "dictated to a scribe, one Fey Li-Wong, in the city of Sian up by the Great Wall." He squinted over the top of his glasses. "This was written more than two months ago."

Tien tai-tai smiled. "I feel my husband is still well." She asked shyly, "Could you write a letter back to him?"

The elder clapped his hands. A maidservant appeared. "Materials."

The girl brought a slate ink-dish and several camel's-hair brushes of various thicknesses. The old man poured a few drops of water onto the slate and ground an ink stick in the water until it was the color he wanted. He smoothed the brush point.

"You were about to say . . . ?"

Tien tai-tai had never before dictated a letter and she was afraid to speak all the things that were in her mind. So she said only a few simple things—that they were well, all of the family; that they were getting along; that every Saturday evening they went to Chin Pi Lu to await Tien's return.

"Please tell our father that Precious Grief is well also," said Chuck.

The elder nodded and sketched the characters for grief, for precious and for good health. Proudly he held up the letter for them to see. His calligraphy was beautiful. The words marched boldly in elegant columns.

Some day I'll write like that, Chuck promised himself.

With great care the elder thumbed open his buffalo-horn chop-box and took out a seal. Chuck noticed the chop was carved out of the best "chicken's blood stone" from Hunan. The top showed a boy sliding off the back of a kneeling elephant. Carefully the elder inked the tip in rich crimson. Carefully he chopped his seal at the left-hand corner of the page. Folding the letter the elder handed it to Tien tai-tai.

"May I pay you?" she offered.

The elder arose and the silken cuffs slid over his clasped hands.

"My small gift," he bowed. "I hope your husband will soon return to his faithful family."

If Tien had only been there, the next month would have been one of the best periods in their lives. The rice bowls were full. Tien tai-tai's purse was getting fatter each day. There was work ahead, at least for a few weeks. Only the shadow of Tien's absence and the money they owed evil old Feng kept them from being completely happy.

They worked hard, day and night, trying always to avail themselves of the friendly wind. For if they had to row their heavy cargos from Cheng-chiang, where the tile was kilned, it was a slow punishing voyage up to Kunming. With a fair wind filling their sail they could reach Kunming's West Gate in eight or ten hours.

Whether it had been an easy week or a hard one, whether the moon were shining or the rain was pouring down, Saturday evenings always found Tien tai-tai and the boys waiting near the chestnut-vendor's stall at Chin Pi Lu Bridge.

TIEN TAI-TAI HAD NEVER DICTATED A LETTER BEFORE.

One night some weeks after the arrival of Tien's letter they were watching the lively evening traffic when Tien tai-tai said wearily, "He'll not come tonight I am sure."

They walked across the bridge to the custom-house gateway which made a cave for them on cold nights.

"Will daddy ever come home?" Pung asked plaintively.

"Certainly he'll come home," Chuck said sturdily. "He'll probably let us play with his rifle and bayonet."

Pung cheered up considerably at that prospect.

This was the beginning of fall and the nights were growing cold so Tien tai-tai laid the quilt on the step and wrapped Pung and Chuck up cocoon fashion. Pung was covered completely, just his eyes peeping out. Chuck, at the other end, didn't have quite so much cover but he was comfortable. Precious Grief, nestling against his neck, helped keep him warm.

Tien tai-tai, with Pung partially on her lap, had only a tattered shawl to keep the top of her warm. But tonight it didn't matter. She was so weary she could have slept in the snow.

Hsun Ching Street where the custom house stood was beyond the city wall. Once it had been the handsomest street in town, lined with villas and gardens backing on the river; a shady street of consulates and government compounds. Hsun Ching Street had changed. Now some of the mansions were cheap hotels and others were gambling dives.

Chuck lay back with his eyes half open watching the occasional rickshaws rattle by and listening to the exciting sounds of muted music and wild laughter. He must have fallen asleep again for he awoke startled by an angry hissing close to his ear. It was Precious Grief.

"Hush," said Chuck. "Latch your beak."

But the cormorant was standing on Chuck's chest, twisting anxiously from side to side, hissing in his throat.

Probably a rat, thought Chuck. He roused himself. The moon had gone. The night was dark. The only sound was the rusty sawing of eucalyptus leaves. Then shadows moved along the river embankment. Two gaunt Lolo tribesmen came slinking along the river side of the street. The slyness of their movements told Chuck that they were up to no good. They disappeared under the arch that led to the river steps.

The skulkers did not reappear but Precious Grief was still restless. His claws twitched and deep in his throat he cackled unceasingly.

"Sleep old water-crow," Chuck urged, grasping the bird by the shag.

The reply was a hiss that would have done justice to a medium-sized dragon. But hardly had the sound died when Chuck heard footsteps. Not the soft slapping of grass sandals, but the bluff tread of foreign boots.

A song lifted through the darkness.

*"Off we go into the wide blue yonder
Riding high into the sun. . . ."*

It was an American singing the Air Force song. No one but an American would be foolish enough to advertise himself in an unlit street at midnight. Chuck was thinking of the stealthy men he'd seen earlier when suddenly he saw two shadows move out from the river gate. He saw two turbaned heads and two crouched bodies. The foolish American was walking into a trap.

Chuck wanted to shout but fear choked him. In the shadows across the way a knife gleamed. That seemed to free the tightness in his throat.

"Wei! Wei!" Chuck yelled.

The tall American turned. For a moment his back was to the river gate.

Swiftly the two Lolos closed in. They came at the tall man like a pair of snow leopards. The American heard the rasp of their sandals and turned. His shoulders dropped a little, ready and loose. The three men came together in a patch of light from a half-shuttered window. There in that midnight pattern the American made his stand.

The battle was brief and silent. The American might have called for help but it would not have done him much good. The Chinese police are early bed-goers. It keeps them out of trouble.

As the killers closed the tall man side-stepped. One arm chopped downwards. The American, using the side of his big hand like a butcher's cleaver, smashed at the footpad's neck. The Lolo hit the cobbles in a heap.

"Ai-yi, ai-yi," he groaned.

The second footpad's knife gleamed in an upswing for the American's stomach. There was the sound of leather ripping as the American moved into the knifeman. He had the heavy agility of a water buffalo. The Lolo was strong too. Chuck could hear them grunt as their bodies locked over the knife. Metal clanged coldly on rock. A knife lay gleaming in the snakeskin pattern of light and darkness. The Lolo swore once in his strange hill-tongue. Then Chuck saw the knifeman twist free and go running after his limping companion. Both disappeared through the river gate.

The American calmly picked up his cap that had rolled off in the fight. He turned toward the gate where Chuck and his mother were standing. Chuck recognized the man. It was his friend, Captain Scott.

"Who was the one who called?" asked Captain Scott. "Who yelled out?"

"I yelled," said Chuck. "The bird woke me."

The flyer grinned. "A regular watchdog, that bird. Here, give him a banquet."

He reached into his pocket, then stopped. "I forgot," he said. "I was playing cards and the boys took me to the cleaner. It would have been quite a joke if those highbinders had knifed me for nothing."

Chuck smiled politely. "Please do not think of money. I warned you because it is bad to stand by and see someone robbed."

The flyer was staring at Chuck and Tien tai-tai where they stood in the shadows. "Aren't you the boat folk?"

"We're the boat family," Tien tai-tai answered.

The tall captain laughed. "You're my luck, that's what you are. I sure appreciate that yell."

Unsnapping an identification disk from his broad wrist, Captain Scott tossed it to Chuck.

"This won't bring much on Silver Street but if you need help take it out to the airfield. One of my men will see the message reaches me wherever I happen to be. Good-bye for now."

"*Tsai chien.*"

The American was off, swinging gaily down the street as if nothing had happened.

Precious Grief was still clucking in remembered anger. Reaching up, Chuck smoothed the cormorant's feathers.

"Let me see the bracelet," Tien tai-tai said curiously.

Chuck handed it to her. It was a silver tag inscribed with writing and numerals and an enameled red, white and blue CBI patch.

"Pretty," said Tien tai-tai.

Chuck smiled. He knew his mother's fondness for trinkets. Pretty it was and it might be useful too.

Chapter Three

SHIPWRECK

F EI-LIEN, God of the Winds, was good to the Tiens. The Chinese have a saying that a thousand strokes with the oar are not equal to a ragged sail. Day after day the Wind God sent his breath from the south helping to move their laden sampan swiftly to Kunming.

One sun-filled morning Chuck awoke and saw his mother emptying the old tobacco pouch she wore under her loose blue coat. She was counting money. Carefully she flattened out the roll of soiled bills bearing Sun Yat Sen's friendly face. Slowly, carefully she counted them one by one.

"Enough?" Chuck asked when she was done.

Tien tai-tai looked startled. "I did not know that you were awake," she said. Her dark eyes crinkled at the corners. "Yes, it's enough. We can buy back our cormorants and have a little to spare."

Chuck threw off the tattered quilt.

"When can we go to Old Feng?"

"Perhaps Saturday when our work is done."

Chuck picked up Precious Grief and hugged him.

"You will soon be with your friends," he said.

Perhaps Precious Grief understood a little of Chuck's happiness, or perhaps he too felt fine that sunlit morning. He burst out in a raucous "haw, haw, haw," which is the cormorant's style of appreciation.

Meanwhile Pung had jumped up from his mat. Hearing the news he commenced jigging around the boat singing, "My birds are coming back. My birds are coming back."

"Look out, Small Son, you'll fall overboard," Tien tai-tai warned.

Pung had hopped to the sampan's narrow pole-walk. Just as his mother spoke he gave a particularly ecstatic leap—and lost his balance. Pung's yelp was only a moment ahead of the splash.

"Again!" said Chuck. He moved quickly to the side of the boat but his mother was faster. She was over the side and had grabbed Pung by his topknot before he had a chance to go down a second time.

"Throw him back in," Chuck said callously. Pung was always falling overboard.

But Tien tai-tai cuddled the squalling Pung until he had gotten over his fright. Then she lifted him into the sampan and, with the aid of Chuck, pulled herself aboard.

"You should have let him stay under a while," Chuck said in brotherly fashion.

Tien tai-tai carefully gathered up the money. Sliding the bills back in the leather pouch she said soberly, "We were unwise to celebrate too soon. Many things could happen."

Steadily, cheerfully they worked the rest of that week ferrying the beautifully glazed jade tile and blue brick to Kunming. But on Saturday the weather changed. Resting on his oar, Chuck watched a four-motored plane from over the Hump heading in. It scarcely moved, fighting the high wind.

"Squall coming," Chuck called back to his mother.

Tien tai-tai was frowning skyward. "Drop sail!" she called.

Running back, Chuck loosed the lines. Down to the deck with a noise like rifle fire rattled the bamboo sail.

Chuck was remembering what his father had done when these sudden squalls struck. He shouted, "Swing into the wind."

Tien tai-tai thrust her weight against the rudder-oar. Slowly the sampan nosed about, pointing its stubby prow into the chop. Waves slapped at the deeply laden craft. The wind cut through Chuck's spray-drenched clothes.

It came without warning, out of the mountains, this quick ferocious storm. Clouds covered the sun, brushstrokes made by a giant hand. But Chuck wasn't watching. Head down he threw all his strength behind each oar-stroke to keep the wallowing sampan slicing the waves. Odd how this peaceful lake, this lake he knew so well, could throw off its disguise and turn into a tiger.

Raising his wet face Chuck looked shoreward. Through the advancing rain he could see willows lined against a point of land.

"Shall we throw the tile overboard?" Chuck shouted anxiously, over his shoulder.

Tien tai-tai heard but shook her head. She was thinking with the Chinese peasant's inborn thriftiness that it would take months to pay back the value of the cargo. She did not stop to consider that she might lose not only the freight but her boat as well.

"Head for shore," she shrieked and the wind made pennants of her black hair.

The shore was coming closer. Up in the prow Chuck could see the low-lying land. He thought he could spot a circular water gate.

Suddenly, above the howling of five thousand devils, Chuck heard a *cra-ack*. Even before he turned he knew what it was. In her hands Tien tai-tai held a broken oar.

"Lash a plank to the oar-peg," Chuck yelled into the wind.

Perhaps Tien tai-tai heard. Perhaps she had already thought of the same device. Quickly she seized a loose board and knotted it to the eight-inch peg. But while she worked the sampan was veering. In spite of Chuck's frantic efforts the boat was swinging broadside to the wind. The sampan dipped like a woman swooning and a wave climbed the low gunwales, the water rolled lazily backwards and forwards. Chuck could feel the coldness as high as his ankles.

"Quick Pung!"

Eyes big, Pung crawled forward. Precious Grief, acting as if he had never in his life been near water, crowded at Pung's legs.

Chuck tied an empty waterkeg under Pung's shoulders. By then the sampan was lurching dangerously. Chuck rose up from where he had placed the whimpering Pung and once more flung his weight against the oar but the sampan was so sluggish, so deep in the water, that it was like a dead thing.

Still they might have gotten close enough to beach the sampan if an extra large wave had not reared up and sent its frothing crest lashing into them. Chuck felt the weight of the water as it poured aboard, felt its sucking swirl as the old craft started to settle. He turned to see his mother's despairing face. She was calling as she made her way along the polewalk.

"Take care of Pung," he thought she said.

Then the sampan started gliding, seemed to be running down hill, and the water closed over Chuck. He felt weeds and saw the strange green under-lake light. Then he was beating his way to the surface.

A wave filled Chuck's mouth. He spat out the water and got a good hold on Pung's keg. Tears from Pung were joining the waters of the lake. Precious Grief was swimming worriedly about, honking loudly. Hearing splashes behind, Chuck twisted around. Tien tai-tai, hampered by her loose clothing, was paddling towards them.

"Are you all right? Is Pung all right?"

"Yes, good," Chuck gurgled.

Tien tai-tai's eyes were still frightened when she reached the boys. "Push towards shore."

When the next wave lifted them, Chuck gazed shoreward. The frantic willows were not far off. Getting behind the buoyant Pung on his keg, Chuck took a deep breath and kicked out. Tien tai-tai was swimming close on Pung's other side. Cackling around them, herding them like a mother duck, was Precious Grief.

The wind was slackening, the waves had less slap. Ahead Chuck saw combs of eel grass. Putting down his legs he tried for the bottom.

"We can stand," he shouted.

Quickly they pushed shoreward. Soon they were able to grasp the dripping willow ends and pull themselves onto the bank. Together Chuck and Tien tai-tai untied Pung.

Pung rubbed his shoulder where the rope had cut into him. "I do not like that storm," he said solemnly.

Chuck smiled a little, glancing up at his mother. And then, for the first time, he realized what the storm had done to them.

Chapter Four

STRANGE REFUGE

TIEN TAI-TAI, one arm around Pung, was gazing out into the wind-slashed lake towards the place where their sampan had sunk. Her eyes were like dim mirrors. Her mouth drooped. All that had been theirs was lost. Their home, their living, even their hope. Now they had no protection against the world. No roof. No means for keeping alive. All that had gone down with their old sampan. All that now lay at the bottom of Tien Chih amid the eel grass.

Tien tai-tai was aware of Pung shivering against her. She saw Chuck's frightened face. For the first time in a life of many hardships Tien tai-tai could not manage a smile.

"Come," she said wearily. Rising, she took Pung's hand in hers while Chuck, cold and frightened, clung to her other side. From a willow branch Precious Grief squawked at having been forgotten. They waited while the silver cormorant flapped down onto Chuck's shoulder. Then they started through the wind-whipped rice paddies towards a cluster of mud houses almost hidden in the pines.

A limping dog came at them viciously out of the rain but they were almost too miserable to care whether he bit or not. They crossed a slab bridge and came into the little square made by the thatched houses. Tien tai-tai knocked at the first nail-studded door. Out of the warm darkness a pigtailed girl stuck her head.

"What do you want?" she asked suspiciously.

Then seeing their shivering coldness she turned her head and called shrilly. A woman came to the door. Her quick black eyes sized up Tien tai-tai and the two boys. The heavy door creaked inwards.

"You have had trouble. Come."

Tien tai-tai stepped into the darkness, Chuck and Pung clinging close to her while Precious Grief darted his head uneasily.

"Our sampan sank. We swam ashore," Tien tai-tai said.

The plump little woman clucked sympathetically.

"Take off your clothes and get dry. I'll warm some noodles and broth."

Crouching close to the brazier, Chuck looked around as he took off his sodden jacket.

Sitting on a low bamboo chair was an old crone, the grandmother of the house. She seemed blind. Beside her stood the little girl, watching them with the eyes of a mouse. Three speckled hens crowded uncomfortably into the single high-up window, and in the far corner, undisturbed, a large sow dreamt pig-dreams.

"You'll feel better after you heat your bellies with this," the woman said briskly, bustling over with three steaming bowls of *mien*.

Tien tai-tai had been so busy drying down the boys that she had scarcely had time to think of herself. Suddenly she gave a gasp.

"The money!"

Everyone in that dank hut stopped what he was doing. Anxiously the whole household watched her reach under her clinging coolie coat and pull forth the tobacco pouch which held the Tien fortune. Hardly breathing they waited for her to open it.

Tien tai-tai, with anxious fingers, undid the drawstrings. Not daring to look she put in her hand and drew out the roll of bills. A soggy mass!

This was too much. Tien tai-tai began to sob. First her husband, then the fishing birds, then her sampan home, and now all the family savings. Fate was bitter. She wept silently. Chuck and Pung, knowing only that they wished they could help, came and stood by their mother.

The farm woman clucked sympathetically. She made signs to the boys to eat their noodles and broth. Then going over to Tien tai-tai she took the mass of soggy paper money out of the boatwoman's lap. Carefully she began to separate the greenish bills. It was like stripping a very wilted head of lettuce. The farm woman laid the money in circles near the brazier.

"They'll dry," she said optimistically.

Tien tai-tai looked up for a moment only to drop her head despairingly. The woman kindly let her weep.

Chuck and Pung ate their noodles. Chives gave the broth

a delicious flavor. When no one seemed to be looking Chuck gave Precious Grief a few noodles. The cormorant liked them and tweaked Chuck's ear for more.

Suddenly the door crashed open as if drawn by the wind. A squat, challenging figure stood in the opening outlined against the slanting rain. Water dripped from his straw hat down over the layers of palm fiber that swathed his shoulders like a cape of reddish monkey fur. He took in Chuck and Pung squatting by the brazier. He took in the silver cormorant crouched on Chuck's shoulder. He noticed the weeping Tien tai-tai. Then his blank black eyes saw the money spread out to dry. His expression did not alter, but Chuck had a moment of fear. Some quiet change had taken place within the man.

"Come," scolded the woman. "Come in, Ho. Come in. Isn't there enough water in the house as it is?"

The man slid in and dropped the rustic cape. He took off his coolie hat and kicked off the mud-soaked sandals. Chuck noticed that a scar ran across the man's shaven scalp down to a point below his jaw.

While the little girl emptied more charcoal into the brazier the woman ladled out hot noodles and handed the bowl to the man. His chopsticks worked as she recounted the Tiens' tragedy. Saying nothing, the man sucked in the noodles. It was the only sound he made.

Except for the woman the whole family seemed afraid of him. In the corner the blind grandmother sat staring down sightlessly at her bound feet in their lotus slippers. Near her stood the little pigtailed girl while the woman of the house washed the bowls and chatted. Tien tai-tai had ceased weeping. She sat quietly between her sons. Pung had begun to take an interest in his surroundings but Chuck was watching the man.

Never once did Chuck surprise an expression on the face of the scar-faced man. When he had finished eating the man stood up. He went to a lacquer chest and took out a pair of dry sandals. Then, without a word, he took hat and cape, opened the creaking door, and stepped out into the darkness.

After he had left there was total silence. Then the woman said, "He was not always like that. He is really not like that now."

No one replied. There seemed nothing to say.

The only light in the earthen-floored hut came from the brazier. It illuminated the edges of things, the rim of a rice bowl, the tip of Tien tai-tai's nose, the chairs polished by many hands. The place was warm and drowsy. The woman yawned. "It's time to sleep. I can give you some mats."

They lay down together, covering almost all the floor space. There was Tien tai-tai and Chuck, with Pung and Precious Grief sandwiched in between. There was the farm woman and her daughter and the grandmother. And there was the pig right in the middle of everything.

Chuck was conscious of his mother glancing towards the drying paper money just before she lay down. The two of them were both thinking the same thought—suspicion was a poor return for hospitality.

Chuck was wondering what the morrow would bring. He was wondering where they would live, how they would eat now that the sampan was down there at the bottom of Tien Chih Lake. Falling asleep he dreamt of the sinister man with the scar carved along one cheek.

Chapter Five

SCARFACE TAKES HIS REWARD

NOT even the hens, high in their window, were stirring when Chuck awakened. Taking Precious Grief in his arms he climbed over Pung and Tien tai-tai. At the door he glanced back. The paper money still lay in a neat circle about the brazier.

Outside Chuck stooped to tie his sandals. Dawn outlined a small threshing ground walled in by the thatched huts. In the center of the little square was a haycock of rice straw. Pine trees bent benignly over the cluster of huts. It was like a miniature village—almost a hidden village, low and secret, walled by willows and pines.

Chuck found an opening between the houses and was soon walking along the dyke that edged the lake. Maybe I can see our sampan, he thought, but he knew that he was hoping against hope. The bricks and tiles would anchor the craft to the bottom.

The storm had passed. The first rays of the sun were like light strained through clear amber. The lake was as smooth as the bottom of a pot.

At the drooping willow where they had come ashore Chuck squatted to gaze across the water. He saw no sign of the sampan.

"Ai—ai," he wailed to himself. "What will we do? Where will we live? What will my father say?"

Then he realized he was staring at a distant stick which stuck up where the sampan had gone down. It looked like the tip of a mast.

It was the mast. The sampan then had gone down in shallow water. Chuck felt a tug of hope but his optimism did not have the strength to flower. With all that tile aboard, the sampan might just as well have sunk in ten fathoms.

Still, a man who is worth his salt does not give up so easily. I must see, Chuck decided none too happily for it was a long swim.

Stripping off his jacket and trousers, Chuck was about to step into the water when a voice startled him.

"Where do you go, boy?"

Chuck turned. The voice belonged to Scarface. He stood at Chuck's shoulder, his hands hidden under his coolie coat. So stealthily had he come up that not even Precious Grief had heard him.

"The boat. I think I can see the mast."

"Ha?"

The unblinking gaze weighed Chuck but told him nothing. Then without more ado the man took off his jacket and trousers and stood bare, squatty and muscular in the kind morning light, and plunged in after Chuck.

The eel grass tickled Chuck's belly. The bolding sun

painted the water in sliding shapes of orange and gold. Precious Grief led the two swimmers, for he was more born to the water than they. Had he not been worried, Chuck would have enjoyed this sunrise swim.

He had hoped that the sampan might have spilled sideways but when he reached the wreck he saw that the craft had settled flat on the bottom. There it sat, distorted by the ripples, seemingly quaking amid the weeds of the lake bottom.

"Not so deep," said Chuck encouraged by the sight of the sampan.

He found he was speaking to lake and sky. Scarface, with a silence typical of all his movements, had dived. Chuck could make out his body palely circling the sampan like a lazy paddlefish.

In a few moments Scarface broke the surface. He didn't say anything, he merely grunted, but Chuck was sure that Scarface figured the sampan could be raised.

They swam ashore. Scarface stopped merely to tie his sandals and britches. Chuck noticed that his feet were horny and cracked like the feet of men who use the mountain trails.

When the silent man had been gone less than a half hour two sampans slanted around the wooded point that screened the houses. The boats came swiftly, poled by expert arms. One sampan swung inshore to pick up Chuck and Precious Grief. Silence seemed to be a habit with these people. The two polers offered not a word.

By the time they reached the sunken sampan the men in the other craft had already lowered a half-dozen five-gallon gasoline tins with open tops and were diving after them. Chuck watched his polers strip off their faded coolie jackets and worn britches. Around each man's waist, stuck in horse-hide belts, were broad Shan knives.

Then it dawned on Chuck. He remembered where he had seen stealthy men like these before. He had seen them trotting at dusk on the edge of the Burma Road, driving weary Mongolian pack-ponies, looking neither to right nor left and yet seeing everything.

"Smugglers," his father had whispered. "Smugglers up from Burma."

That was it; these men were smugglers. Back there in the pines was a smugglers' village. That was the reason for their odd silence. Chuck's relief gave way to worried suspicion.

Some of that creepy silence fled as the men dived and splashed, loading the underwater harvest into the big tins to be pulled aboard the anchored sampans.

"Is it gold you dive for? Or pearls?" one man joked.

"Pretty big pearls," another answered, holding up a tile.

They actually laughed at Precious Grief. Inspired by the sight of men diving like cormorants Precious Grief was outdoing himself. He brought up everything he could find. A pewter spoon. Tien tai-tai's beads. A little painted wooden dragon belonging to Pung. Several times he caught a carp and swam with it, flopping in his beak, to Chuck. Once while they were resting, Precious Grief stayed under so long that Chuck grew worried. Finally the silver cormorant surfaced in a fountain of spray. His captive, a barred loach, long and narrow, was almost as large as its captor.

Precious Grief held the flipping giant halfway down its back. The whiskered loach fought hard, dragging the cormorant under. But Precious Grief kept his beak clamped, working his prize towards the boats.

"Hold him, water-tiger!" The men called encouragement.

"Don't let him drown you!"

Finally the fish weakened and Precious Grief proudly paddled to Chuck. He could not lift his heavy prize. Chuck slipped his fingers under the loach's gills and pulled it aboard.

Scarface nodded, showing his first human sign.

"A good hunter, that one."

Chuck was amazed at the quiet efficiency of the smugglers. Before the sun was halfway to noon the sunken craft had been stripped of its cargo. All the tile and brick had been ferried ashore and piled neatly under the willows. Of course some of the cargo and family possessions were scattered among the weeds but the main thing was the sampan itself. As Chuck poled back towards the spot where the mast rose lonesomely he prayed that the sampan could be raised. So much in the lives of his family depended upon it. But Chuck had the feeling that even if the smugglers did succeed in raising the sampan, his own troubles were far from over. There was no trusting these men, no trusting them even a trifle.

Scarface directed the salvaging with the aid of a spidery oldster who had the scarred thumbs and competent ways of a carpenter.

"A line under the stern ... A line under the bow," Scarface commanded.

Eight feet below, the divers worked methodically. Chuck watched them slip the grass ropes beneath the sampan's prow. Working a line under the stern was harder because of the slant of the lake bottom. But they made it. With arms and legs waving like tentacles the divers fashioned a rope cradle.

They brought the two lines to the surface and made them fast to the thwarts of the two sampans.

"You think she'll rise?" Chuck asked anxiously.

"Don't ask me, ask the gods," grunted Scarface.

Chuck turned away. Staring downwards, he watched the water slowly clear. Bubbles were bursting through the water-weeds. Fish, too small to interest Precious Grief, darted among the swaying plants, shooting in and out of the sampan. The fish are trying to take the boat over, thought Chuck. And they might end by getting it.

"Ready brothers!"

Scarface's men—brothers by birth or profession, Chuck was not sure which—rose lightly, bamboo poles cocked. Not counting Chuck, there were three polers to each sampan. They let the two boats drift apart until the ropes grew taut. Then, setting their poles, the men bent to their task. It was a tug-of-war, broadside to broadside, with the Tien sampan, like a sick monster, hugging the bottom.

"Ai-yi-yi," chanted the polers. "Ay-yi-yi."

Never in his life had Chuck poled harder. Never before had he made less headway. Nothing happened. The sampan seemed to have dug in.

"Hold," said Scarface.

The men eased up.

"Slack off."

The sampans drifted. Chuck watched the smuggler's face. He did not trust Scarface, yet he felt the man knew what he was doing.

A calculating look showed through Scarface's mask. "The mud's holding her," he told the carpenter. "Give the boat a nudge."

Chuck added his pole to the carpenter's but he could feel no give. It was hard to see what was happening for the water was dirtier than an ink-fish's mess.

Then Chuck's heart leapt, for the tiniest lift telegraphed itself up the long bamboo. The carpenter must have sensed it too for he hissed with pleasure.

"Now!" Scarface snarled.

The sampans slid crabwise. Bamboos dug into the lake bottom. Lines grew taut. Chuck felt the craft beneath him dip as he pushed with every last ounce. Bubbles broke the surface and a lot of mud came up.

"More . . . more . . . more," singsonged Scarface.

Chuck felt the craft jerk beneath him as the sunken sampan commenced to rise. To Chuck it seemed hours before the ribs of the familiar cabin rose above the lake. Then with a rush the sampan surfaced, showed her muddy nose.

"Bail," ordered Scarface as the waterlogged sampan tried to settle again.

Chuck grabbed a pail and jumped overboard. A man from the other boat was already at work.

Hooking one arm over the side where the gunwale barely broke the lake surface, Chuck worked like mad. He bailed until his calloused hands were raw but he didn't notice the pain much for his sampan was rising. Inch by inch she was steadying above the water. It was a wonderful thing for Chuck. He knew though that Scarface had to be reckoned with before the sampan would again be his. Chuck had no illusions about Scarface. The smuggler was doing this for a price.

It didn't take long after that. Chuck and Scarface were soon poling the Tien sampan towards the point of pines. The other boats had gone ahead.

"Hao! Hao!"

Shouts and cheers from a dozen watchers greeted them as they put into the creek. Chuck waved to his mother and Pung.

"Good son," called Tien tai-tai.

Chuck smiled. He wanted to feel thankful and happy but he was almost as anxious as when the sampan lay sunk there on the lake bottom.

People crowded aboard as soon as they tied up.

"The boat needs scrubbing but it seems sound," said Tien tai-tai cheerfully.

"Look at the fish," squeaked Pung.

Chuck grinned. "Precious Grief was busy. There are always lots of fish after a storm."

Chuck had passed a willow through the gills of the largest loach. He wanted to make Scarface a present. One way or the other it was the thing to do. But Scarface was not in sight. The smuggler's sudden disappearance was another barb of worry to Chuck.

"What are you waiting for? Help me clean up," scolded Tien tai-tai happily.

Chuck stripped off his damp jacket and went to work. The sun was comfortingly warm and soon Chuck forgot his worries.

"I wish we hadn't lost our brazier," complained Tien tai-tai, forgetting she had almost lost everything.

"It's not lost," said Chuck. "It's back with the tiles."

"The people of this village are indeed kind," said Tien tai-tai.

Chuck went on scrubbing. He had straightened up to rest when he saw Scarface leaning against one of the pines. The man's face showed nothing, neither friendliness nor dislike, nor even interest, but Chuck knew he was watching and waiting.

"I might as well find out his price," thought Chuck.

He stepped ashore, walking slowly towards Scarface, carrying his offering. Precious Grief, complaining at being left, hopped at Chuck's heels.

Chuck stopped in front of Scarface. "My mother and I want you to have this fish. We are grateful for the way you have helped us," Chuck said with a formality learned from watching elders.

Scarface's only answer was the soft burble of his water pipe. From a buffalo-hide pouch he plucked a bit of thinly shredded tobacco and thumbed it into the clay bowl.

Scarface said, "Much work. Much time. Therefore much pay."

The fish was heavy in Chuck's hands. "How much do we owe you?"

Scarface's eyes were mocking when he spoke the sum.

"What!" Chuck said.

Scarface repeated.

It was almost exactly, to the last *yuan*, all that the Tien family had saved. It was almost as if Scarface had somehow, in the darkness, counted their money.

Chuck's small assurance deserted him. "We can't pay that."

"Why?"

"That's all we have."

"The sampan is worth more."

"More, yes. But without the sampan we couldn't live."

"So the sum is fair," Scarface said without shifting his unblinking gaze.

"But how will we get back our fishing birds?" Chuck asked, and there was a quaver in his voice.

Scarface almost showed surprise. "Back from where?"

"Back from Old Feng."

A dragon's wreath of smoke burst from Scarface's flat nose. "Feng!" he said harshly. "Feng of the Buzzards?"

"He lent us rice money and took our seven cormorants so we'd be sure to pay him back. If we can't pay before another month goes by, he'll get Precious Grief in the bargain. That's what we promised."

The smuggler nodded. His scar twisted into a tart smile.

"Feng of the Buzzards," he said. "Yes, that sounds like Old Feng—buzzard, serpent, centipede and toad all in one."

The smuggler arose. Chuck was more frightened by the smile on that grim face than he had been by its somberness.

"I'm hardly the man to squeeze Feng's victims," said Scarface. "Here, boy, give me the fish and take your sampan."

Before Chuck could speak, the scarfaced one had turned and was walking back among the pines. Chuck would have liked to run after him and thank him but he feared Scarface might change his mind.

The Tiens were grateful for their good luck. Had they been religious folk they would have burnt punks to Fei Lien, God of the Winds, for having driven their sampan into shallow water. As it was they thanked all the gods in their hearts.

"We lost many things in the sinking," said Tien tai-tai. "We won't be able to buy back our cormorants just yet."

Chuck nodded. He was used to misfortunes. This was just a temporary setback.

Chapter Six

A LONG ARM REACHES

 S ATURDAY came quickly that week as it always does when a lot has been happening. As usual Tien tai-tai left the sampan in charge of some of the boat tribe and trudged towards Chin Pi Lu.

It was a lovely summer evening. The setting sun had stormed the ancient city walls with burning color. Overhead white egrets made their odd journey away from the peaceful lake to perch in the palace gardens in the middle of the town. This was the kind of evening that Tien had loved best. He liked to smoke and watch the clouds. He would quote from his handed-down knowledge of the sages: "An inch of time on the sundial is worth more than an inch of gold."

Chuck wondered, would his father ever come back? Would he ever sit there quoting his proverbs? While Tien

"YOU ARE THE FAMILY TIEN?"

had been with them no times had seemed too bad. Now nothing seemed particularly good. There was a saying that woman needs a husband and sons need a father, and it was true.

Evening found Tien tai-tai, Chuck and Pung at their usual stand by the chestnut-vendor's booth. They had hardly gotten there when they saw a soldier limping down the street. Even in the cryptic lantern-light Chuck noticed that the man had lost a leg. One trouser was pinned up and he was using a willow-fork for a crutch.

"Look," Chuck said.

"I see," said his mother in a frightened voice.

"Father?"

"No. Not even war could have changed him that much."

The soldier approached. He stopped before the Tiens, leaning tiredly on his crutch.

"You are the family Tien?" he asked courteously.

"We are that family," said Tien tai-tai, trying to restrain her eagerness.

The soldier looked away from Tien tai-tai's hopeful face. Even here, where the town dwindled, crowds of peddlers and coolies shuffled in and out. It was a poor place to speak of life and death but some things cannot wait.

"I saw Tien three weeks ago just before I left Chengtu. He was in the hospital."

Tien tai-tai's face had lost its brief joy. Her cheeks, in the dim light, were waxen like old gardenia petals.

"What happened to Tien?"

"A head wound. He did not know me though I'd been his comrade for many months."

"Will he get better?" Tien tai-tai begged as if the one-legged soldier could help.

"I don't know," the soldier said matter-of-factly, his sad eyes returning to her face. "They said he might get better, he might get worse, they didn't know. Nobody knows."

Tien tai-tai felt her two sons pressing close to her. She remembered her courtesy. This poor soldier had troubles of his own yet he had come to find her and give her what news he could.

"Thank you," she said. "How did you know where to find us?"

The soldier smiled. "That was easy. When we talked Tien always used to tell how you and his sons would be waiting each Saturday at Chin Pi Lu Bridge. I knew you the moment I saw you."

Tien tai-tai dropped her face to hide her tears.

"Good-bye," said the soldier. "I did what I could. Tien would have done the same for me."

They watched him swing across the bridge, their last link with Tien who was wounded and sick in far-off Chengtu.

Hope seemed to have suddenly gone out of their lives, as if swept away like a chicken crate on the back of a Yellow River flood. I'll never see my father again, thought Chuck. All these nights of waiting and now he'll never come.

"Is daddy hurt?" asked Pung. "Is he coming soon?"

Tien tai-tai's eyes glistened with tears.

"We must go to him. We must find him. We could make him well again," she said stoutly.

"But how?" asked Chuck. "Chengtu is far. Almost to Tibet."

"Far by road, yes. But if we could go by air . . ." She

touched the silver disc on Chuck's wrist. "Perhaps the American would help us."

"The American. The red one!" Chuck had a wonderful moment of hope.

"We'll go to the airfield," said Tien tai-tai decisively.

"What if the American flyer isn't there?"

" 'He who stands still in mud sticks in it,' " quoted Tien tai-tai, remembering one of her husband's sayings.

They plodded down the same road taken by Tien. Tired little Pung took turns riding Chinese-fashion, first on his mother's back and then on Chuck's. The shops and small houses thinned out. The Eastern Bell Tower fell behind. Mustard fields gleamed in the moonlight like gold-streaked mandarin robes. The road ran rough but straight under the ghostly mulberry trees.

At midnight they stopped beside a farmhouse. Tien tai-tai, the boys, and Precious Grief dozed, huddled together for warmth like a covey of quail. Long before sunup they were on the road again, clopping along steadily on their straw sandals. Across the dark fields they could hear the drone of warming planes.

A coolie showed them where the flyers lived. He pointed out a yellow compound emblazoned with the blocky blue character for China. It was vast, filled with tired-looking mud buildings left over from the Fourteenth Air Force. No one had seen Captain Scott. Finally a mechanic pointed out the control tower.

Tien tai-tai and the two boys plodded around the great air-strip that had once seen hundreds of planes a day—now it was like a dusty chariot-field of some half-forgotten civilization. Only a handful of planes dotted the magnificent emptiness. Sunflowers grew in the revetments.

"Captain Scott . . . He left a week ago," a willowy CNAC pilot told Tien tai-tai in a Peiping accent. "He's up north somewhere."

It was a black moment for the Tiens for they had counted on the flyer's knowledge of the world outside as well as his help. Tien tai-tai was disappointed but she was a proud and stubborn woman. "We have money," she said to Chuck. "We can buy tickets."

Chuck's black eyes sparkled. "Let's go right away. I'll find out how much it costs."

The price turned out to be startling. The Tiens were simple people. Riches to them meant a sampan, plenty of rice, some warm clothes and a little money. Planes belonged to a different world.

"Just one ticket will take almost all we've saved," Chuck told Tien tai-tai desperately, when the scholarly clerk had checked the fare to Chengtu.

Tien tai-tai looked beaten. The money meant so much. It meant getting back the cormorants. It meant food and security, but she said firmly, "Your father needs us. He needs the family." She put a hand on Chuck's shoulder. "Since we can only get one ticket you, Eldest Son, must go."

Suddenly the world seemed vast to Chuck. In all his twelve years he had never been more than ten miles from his native lake. The thought of going to a strange, far city frightened him.

"I don't want to go, Mother."

Tien tai-tai smiled. "I must stay and take care of little Pung. You must help your father."

"Alone?"

"You could take Precious Grief."

Chuck felt a little better. Precious Grief was part of the family. Going to the desk he asked the spectacled clerk if he could take the cormorant along.

The wizened clerk eyed Precious Grief with a marked lack of enthusiasm.

"Cormorants are notoriously dirty."

"Not this one."

"I shall peruse the regulations. Let me see, birds . . . birds . . . birds . . . chickens . . . no . . ."

After five minutes the man looked up wearily from his regulation book. He glanced coldly at Precious Grief astride Chuck's shoulder.

"Nothing whatsoever concerning cormorants," he said resignedly. "Presumably one can take such a bird though I do not endorse the concept."

Precious Grief, who could always tell who liked him and who didn't, leaned over and, fixing the clerk with a foxy eye, cawed like a fat crow.

The Chengtu flight was scheduled for the next morning, which was fortunate, for it only left once a week. Chuck wished that the day would pass swiftly. If he waited too long he feared his courage would ebb.

A strange thing happened next morning while the Tiens squatted in the early sunlight eating their breakfast rice. Two rickshaws pulled into the CNAC compound. In the lead rode Feng of the Buzzards.

As he stepped creakily from the buggy his good eye, as if by chance, lighted on the patient Tiens.

"Ah so," said Feng. "My cormorant friends." He showed his toothless gums. "You are perhaps going on a journey?"

Tien tai-tai gave him back look for look. "My husband is ill. The boy is going to Chengtu to bring him home."

"Ah so! Most lamentable. I hope your son is not taking along the silver cormorant."

"The bird's going with him," Tien tai-tai said.

Rage gleamed in Feng's good eye.

"This we do not allow. Remember the silver cormorant is pledged to me."

Tien tai-tai, still squatting, brought her firm gaze to bear on Feng's droop-lidded face.

"Pledged, yes. But the bird's not yours unless we fail to pay our debt by the end of six more weeks."

Old Feng changed his tune. He became the courtier, his voice and manner dripping with *kuchi*.

"The wise Mencius said, 'Better take eight hundred cash than to give credit for a thousand.' Plane trips are dangerous and I would not like to risk losing this bird. Suppose I give you back your other seven fishing birds and pay you a hundred gold in addition. All this in exchange for the silver cormorant."

It was a good offer. Tien tai-tai turned her questioning gaze on Chuck. He looked scared and desperate. Tien tai-tai shook her head.

"No."

"Ah so!" hissed old Feng. "Well, keep your bird for a few more weeks, woman. I shall have him and the others too. Mencius said, 'Hunger is cured by food, ignorance by study.' But you don't seem to learn, and you may soon know hunger."

Tien tai-tai arose. "I'm not fat with the wisdom of the ancients, Old Man," she said. "But I remember one saying my father valued: 'Injure others—injure yourself.' Remember that, Old Man."

She walked away, Chuck and Pung trailing after her.

If they had turned they might have seen Old Feng talking with the man in the second rickshaw, a man whose brawny shoulders overloaded the blue scholar's gown he uncomfortably wore. He was the type known in some of the less civilized parts of the Celestial Kingdom as a hatchet man.

"I must have this cormorant," Feng said briefly. "Those stupid coolies don't know it, but the bird is worth his weight in dragon-jade."

The big man's face was a smooth and shiny mask. Not even his lips moved when he answered.

"Have I ever failed you?"

Feng cackled. "You know better than to fail me, Mister Lung."

"Go back to your bird-droppings," Lung said sullenly. "I will handle this business of a weak boy and that hook-billed humming bird."

Chapter Seven

HOW FENG CAME TO CLAIM PRECIOUS GRIEF

T HE battered C47 with the sweeping characters of China National Airways emblazoned on its side beat the air with twin motors as it warmed up for the take-off. Chuck felt caught within a frenzied cage. Precious Grief cackled, clamping tighter to Chuck's shoulder. It was like being in the racking center of a typhoon until the pilot freed his brakes and gave the old crate the gun. The C47 swept down the crushed-rock runway, bounced a couple of times, and took-off.

Chuck peered through the window. The red Yunnanese earth fell away. He strained for a last look at Tien tai-tai and Pung but they were already many *lis* behind. Only Lake Tien Chih was recognizable. He could see junks and sampans, silver toys on a slate slab. Fast, fast, fast he was leaving everything familiar to him. It was a lonely thought.

"I'm going to meet my father," he told himself. "I'm the eldest son, I'm a man almost."

The C47 banked and nosed northwards. Below, the dragon peaks of the Himalaya foothills sprawled in lazy loops.

This cloud voyage to the sampan boy, who never had been farther than a few miles from the lake, who had never ridden in a car or seen a tall building, was like being carried into the future.

Chuck was scarcely conscious of the other passengers—the Chinese general, the pale missionary lady, the Moslem merchant, and the man in the too-tight scholar's gown.

The drone of the twin motors, the warmth, the motion, drugged Chuck's senses. He found himself thinking of things in the past. He found himself remembering the day that he and Pung and Tien tai-tai had gone to Feng and the old man had maneuvered them into mortgaging the cormorants. He remembered the coffin.

It had started with the rains. Every summer the monsoon whips southwest China but this summer the rains held a fury that amounted to hate. The roads became wrinkles of red mud. Lake Tien Chih was striped with silt. Farmers ferried themselves around their farmyards while their hens tried to lay eggs on walls and sloping roofs.

Rivers and canals poured mud into the lake until the cormorants were diving in darkness. Even though the Tiens worked from dawn until dusk they often failed to catch a single fish. Pung lost his chubby look. Chuck's skin hung loose around his belly from lack of food and Tien tai-tai's blue coat and pantaloons flapped on her gaunt frame.

"What can we do?" Tien tai-tai spoke hopelessly one evening. "There's nothing to eat and nothing to buy food with."

His mother had sold her silver earings and bracelets weeks ago, Chuck knew. Everything worth selling had been sold. He thought he knew what was in his mother's mind.

"The fishing birds?"

Tien tai-tai did not answer. She gazed across the lake as if distance was a release.

"How will we make a living after they're gone," Chuck demanded.

Tien tai-tai regarded her calloused hands. "The birds will bring a good price even in these bad times. We'll eat for a while. We'll do whatever comes along. We should be able to make enough to buy back Tien's cormorants."

"And father," Chuck accused, "what will he say when he finds we've sold his fishing birds?"

"I don't know."

"Well, maybe the rains will stop," Chuck said, wanting to put off the final reckoning.

But the rains did not stop. Day after day they slanted down with an end-of-the-world fury.

After one particularly unending spell Tien tai-tai looked at her pinch-faced sons and made up her mind. Swinging the tiller she ran through the scudding downpour that drove westwards towards Hsi Shan and a forbidden section of the lake called Smugglers' Cove. She was headed for the old man who bought and sold and lent money on birds, the strange old man called Feng of the Buzzards.

Oddly as they approached the west shore the rain died and the sun came out. Tien tai-tai was almost tempted to put about and try once more but she knew it would take a good week for the water to clear. By then Chuck and Pung would be too thin to stand. She couldn't face their pinched faces any more nor listen to their hungry whimperings at night.

As the sampan nosed in towards the dark curve of land that formed the cove, Chuck and Pung came back to speak with her. They held their pet, the silver cormorant, between them.

"You won't sell Precious Grief? We couldn't get along without Precious Grief."

Tien tai-tai stared sadly at her two boys with the big white bird clutched in their arms. Precious Grief must have known something was up for he huddled, head flat as a snake's, under Chuck's arm. Pung was anxiously petting Precious Grief's ducklike rump.

The tight lines around their mother's eyes relaxed a little. She smiled but it was a sad smile. "Precious Grief is one of the family," she said. Perhaps she had forgotten that in times of China's famines people had been known to sell part of their family so that the rest might live.

Putting the cormorants into baskets, Tien tai-tai slung them on opposite ends of a carrying-pole. She pattered off with a springy gait that kept the load bouncing. Chuck and Pung followed with Precious Grief riding like a feathered king on Chuck's shoulder.

As the Tiens approached the crackling eucalyptus grove at the foot of West Mountain they were met by a festival of sounds. From among the guano-splashed trees came the hissing of Peking geese, the lilting of a thrush, crows cawing and the cackling of zebra parakeets. Pigeons with bamboo whistles attached to their legs swirled among the branches with a sighing sound. In hanging cages, fortuneteller birds chirped optimistically, and somewhere off amongst the trees a peacock screamed. Over and under these sounds came the tinkling of wind chimes.

Men, heavily bandollered and armed with rifles, stepped from behind the trees and stopped the Tiens. Tien tai-tai told them her business and one of the guards crunched off to find Feng.

To Chuck it seemed odd that a dealer in birds would live like a war lord but these were troubled times. Perhaps Feng of the Buzzards needed guards for he was known to be rich and cruel and many people owed him money.

Chuck had heard tales of Feng. He knew he was old but he was startled when he saw the man. Feng came tottering down the path over the crinkled carpet of eucalyptus bark, his head as weazened as the meat of a litchi nut. He was so old that he looked cold even in the sunlight. He was the oldest man that Chuck had ever seen, and the most evil.

Tien tai-tai slipped the carrying-pole from her shoulder and placed the cages in front of Feng.

"I have some cormorants."

Feng of the Buzzards bowed, his dark eye observing the caged birds while the milky one gazed blindly ahead.

"Ah so," he hissed. "The birds of Tien."

"How did you know?" Tien tai-tai asked wonderingly. She had never seen Feng before.

"I know every strain of cormorant in Yunnan," Feng said. His good eye rested avariciously on Precious Grief. He added softly, "But I don't know the silver bird. I would not have thought to see one like that in this out-of-the-way province."

Tien tai-tai said quickly, "We've had him several years. He's the family pet."

"Ah so," said Feng. He drew an ivory fan from his sleeve, clicking it open and shut with an elaborate rhythm.

"Follow please."

He led them through the resounding grove to a teak table that stood in a clearing. Farther back was a cave that must have been Feng's living quarters. The entrance was covered with a scarlet hanging on which was embroidered the figure of Chang Kuo-lao, one of the eight Taoist immortals.

As usual in pictures and embroideries the jolly old god was carrying a bamboo-tube drum and riding a white mule. Legend ascribed to Chang the power of folding up the white mule like paper and putting it away in his purse. When Chang wanted to ride he poured water into the purse and the mule reappeared. Chang was naturally one of the boys' favorite gods. They were a little surprised that Feng approved of the cheerful Chang.

A sullen coolie, who looked more like a bandit, brought boiling water to Feng who poured it into a rare blue willow tea pot. No one spoke until the tea was brewed. Feng poured a cup for Tien tai-tai but his single eye was everywhere, particularly upon Precious Grief.

Feng said, "You wish to sell me something, is that so?"

Tien tai-tai nodded away the boys. As they walked away they heard her say, "I have heard that you lend money on fishing birds. I would like to leave mine with you in return for a loan . . ."

Chuck and Pung were glad to get away. The grove was full of birds, some in cages, a few merely tied by long cords to their natural perches in the lower branches of the trees. One huge wicker cage was filled with rare white-headed bulbuls, flycatchers, hoopoes, Burmese cuckoos, Sultan tits, green pigeons, white parakeets, and other birds that the boys had never before seen. Pung was fascinated by the arrogant Bengal fighting cocks that strutted, all scarlet and black and gold. Chuck was more interested in a small black ironwing that had the freedom of the grove. Inquisitively the bird tried landing on Chuck's head but Precious Grief hissed him off. Chuck tossed a bit of bark and the ironwing swooped it up in midair.

"Ironwings are like tigers," Chuck said. "They're not even afraid of hawks."

"I'd rather be a hawk," said Pung practically.

They had approached the cave which was obviously Feng's living quarters and, since the Chang Kuo-lao hanging was partially pulled aside, they glanced in. The cave was furnished with great richness, with Oman rugs, with teakwood tables and chairs glistening with mother-of-pearl. But what caught the boys' eyes was a sumptuous black and gold chest the size of a skiff that held the place of honor in the center of the gaudy cavern.

"What's that?" whispered Pung, though he knew what it was.

"The old man's coffin. Some people like to have a coffin ready when they die."

Fascinated by the coffin, Pung had stepped into the cave to inspect it.

"Come back," Chuck urged. "Old Feng might catch you and nail you under the lid."

But Pung's curiosity had always been a size too large for him. The coffin was so beautiful he had to touch it, to feel its smoothness and its embracing shape. He had just lifted the cover and was peeping in when a vicious voice froze him.

"Child devil! Son of a turtle," screamed old Feng. "Get away from my coffin. Get away, you scavenger."

Pung dropped the lid and hid his face. Chuck, too, ducked under from the old man's fury. Feng's lips were drawn back from toothless gums and he seemed like a hating animal, or perhaps like a buzzard without a buzzard's calmness. He raked at Pung with those talon-hands but Pung had been watching and he jumped away from Feng. Only Tien tai-tai seemed strong in the face of Feng's madness.

"He meant no harm. He's only a child," she said, putting an arm in front of Pung.

"Child or not, he shouldn't have touched the coffin of Feng. In the old days in Peking I'd have had him tossed on the spears."

Tien tai-tai cast Feng of the Buzzards a look that, for her, was ferocious. She brushed by, one son at each side, past the wrathful old man and his gaudy coffin.

When they were down at the lake again, Chuck, who had been observing his mother, asked the dreaded question.

"He didn't make you give him Precious Grief, did he?"

For a moment Tien tai-tai avoided his eyes. Finally she gathered her courage, and it took more courage to face her sons than it had to face old Feng.

"We have three months to pay him back."

"What if we can't pay?" asked Chuck.

"Then we must give him Precious Grief, too," Tien tai-tai said in a choking voice. "That's the only way he would have it."

Chapter Eight

ON THE CHENGTU ROAD

THE sun was an hour past noon when the C47 bumbling over the emerald rice paddies of Szechwan province, began to drop down. Clusters of mud houses in their curving pattern of green rice paddies tilted closer. Suddenly the C47's motors cut out and Chuck looked about wildly. They were dropping uncomfortably fast.

Across from him the general's face was passive like the face of a warrior on an ancient scroll. That was the way a general would die. But the missionary lady too seemed relaxed in her safety belt. A woman wouldn't die so manfully.

The plane leveled. A runway flashed alongside. Bump. The screech of rubber. Another bump and the plane settled like a reluctant air devil.

"We're here," Chuck told Precious Grief softly, looking down at the air-sick bird nestling in his lap.

Chuck stood on the edge of the crushed-rock airstrip wondering in which direction lay Chengtu. He could see no city. Only the vast field and the hills. Precious Grief sidled nervously on his shoulder.

A jeep came to meet the general. The missionary lady was greeted by two beaming friends. Most of the other passengers wandered across to where a charcoal-burning bus sat beside the shabby air terminal.

"Where're you going, junior birdman?" a jaunty CNAC pilot stopped to ask.

"To Chengtu."

"It's a long way afoot. Thirty-five miles."

Thirty-five miles! Chuck had little money left and what he had he would need.

"Where's the road?"

The pilot waved his cigarette. "Across the strip. Straight east. You can't miss it."

The flyer was right, Chuck had no trouble finding the road. It was a narrow highway, lined with dusty poplars. On each side fields of grain and rape spread endlessly. This was green country, brilliantly green and gray, with none of the friendly red of the Yunnanese earth. But the solid road underfoot felt good.

Once Chuck had left the airfield behind, he passed a string of jingling pack-ponies paced by turbaned drivers who neither looked nor sounded Chinese. He passed several two-wheeled carts dragged by men in place of ponies. The people here were even poorer than in Yunnan, yet the country looked richer.

It was a fine afternoon, fresh and clear, and Chuck strode along whistling a fisherman's chanty. He would not have felt so easy if he had recognized the man trailing half-a-mile behind. Mr. Lung had discarded his presumptuous scholar's gown for a peasant coat which more easily concealed the German automatic under his armpit. Lung was happy too in his peculiar way. His simple plan was set. With the coming of darkness the road would be deserted. He would creep up on Chuck, silence him, and steal the cormorant. Quickly he would have the bird in the hands of Feng. The old man was camel-mean but he rewarded those who served him.

The afternoon was getting on when Chuck came around a bend and saw the bogged-down cart. Here a stream crossed the road leaving a platter of silt. The cart, laden with pea-sized coal, was in deep. There was no pony to drag it out, only a ewe-necked man and two children.

Chuck stopped and watched the carter make a desperate effort but the man already wore the look of defeat. The boy and the girl, who weren't much older than Pung, seemed too weary to care. At first Chuck wondered why they didn't unload the cart but it was obvious that if they dumped the pea-coal it would all be lost in the silt. Unloading it basket by basket, and carrying it to high ground, would be a heart-breaking job.

Once again the man and the children heaved, knee-deep in the yellow muck. The cart moved a little and was sucked back.

"Wait," said Chuck, lifting Precious Grief off his shoulder. "Let me help."

The carter, more bent from work than from age, eyed Chuck dubiously but gladly handed him a tug-line. Then the four of them threw their shoulders into the harness. Perhaps Chuck's fresh strength made the difference. Perhaps it

was merely his friendly help. At any rate the cart began to
move.

"Wei, wei," grunted the carter. "Wei, wei, wei."

The crooked cart lurched on its straw-stuffed auto tires,
lurched and came free with a sucking sound. Slowly but
steadily it began to move through the silt. After they had
rolled a hundred feet to where the road was good the carter
called a halt. With his hands on his weary back he smiled
at Chuck.

"I owe you much thanks, boy."

"A small thing," Chuck said politely.

"To us it meant much," replied the man truthfully.

"Let me help a while."

The carter's dusty eyes brightened. "Another shoulder
is always welcome."

To tell the truth, not generosity alone had prompted
Chuck. The sun was edging down. Night was ready to drop
over this house-empty land which in ancient times, and times
not so ancient, had been the scene of so many raids and bat-
tles that even now the people lived in walled villages and
towns. Precious Grief sensed the loneliness and edged closer
to Chuck's neck.

For perhaps half an hour, while sunset streamers blazoned
the sky, Chuck helped the carter and his children haul the
cart. Darkness brought them to the edge of a village.

"Enough for one day," grunted the carter.

Close to the crumbling walls they unharnessed themselves.
From a battered box the carter brought a sack of rice. Meas-
uring out a cupful he gave it to his daughter. Then the
carter unlashed the cook-pot from the axle.

"You must eat with us," he invited.

Chuck hesitated. These people seemed poorer even than his own family. Still the invitation sounded well-meant and Chuck was lonely and cold and tired.

"I'll stay."

The people in the north cooked much as they did at home, Chuck found from watching the girl. With larklike movements she dusted off the utensils using a bamboo brush. Into the boiling water she lowered her little drum of rice. When the rice was done she carefully drained it. She emptied the rice water and dropped a speck of pork into the pot. A few bamboo sprouts and wilted dandelion greens followed. It was a simple meal but to Chuck, who had not eaten since dawn, it tasted like a feast.

Chuck and the carter chatted while the carter's young son squatted silently by, listening with admiring curiosity. When Chuck had finished the story of how he had come all the way from Kunming to look for his father the carter nodded. "You're a good son so you must have a good father. If there is virtue in heaven you will succeed."

"Is Chengtu a big city?" Chuck asked.

"A big city. A great city," the Szechwanese answered, proudly. "In the days of the Three Kingdoms it was a capital. But long ago the Tartars came and took the city. They pulled down the palace, all but the outside wall. Now in the middle of the city, where once lived the king and his court, there is only a gateway to nothing. To cabbage fields."

Until the moon rose they stirred the fire and talked. Then the carter motioned to the holes that pocked the village walks like black cavities at the base of decaying teeth.

"The dawns here are sometimes cold," said the carter. "These little caves make good cocoons."

Taking Precious Grief under his arm Chuck went into the nearest of the burrows. The carter and his family found a slightly larger cave nearby. With Precious Grief nestled close Chuck soon fell asleep on the straw left by a previous traveler. It had been a day of strange journeying and he was hugely tired.

Chapter Nine

FENG'S HIRED ASSASSIN

Down the road just a piece slept another traveler. Oddly enough he slumbered well and peacefully, the kind of sleep generally attributed to the innocent and just. Perhaps the conscienceless also sleep well at times.

But when the moon leaned low at that time preceding the dawn, sometimes called the hour of the huntsman, Lung awoke. Immediately he was alert. He arose and started up the road towards the village. As he approached the cart he halted and stood listening. His brutish face, turned towards the honeycombed walls, was as expressionless as a carp's.

Nothing stirred. No watchman walked the crumbling battlements. No wind rustled the giant bamboos. From the broad belt at his waist Lung slipped a noosed cord. From his shoulder scabbard of smelly Chinese leather he slid the Luger, holding it by the barrel like a club. Stealthily, feel-

ing his way on bare feet, he moved towards the cave where
Chuck slept with Precious Grief in his arms.

If a man of Chengtu had been watching he would have
been reminded of the King of the Cats, that household deity
of the ancient city. There was a stillness about Lung, a
smoothness in his movements, that belongs to animals that
hunt at night.

Swiftly Lung crossed to the shadow of the walls. For a
moment he paused at the cave mouth to rehearse his plan.
First a blow for the boy. Then the loop over the bird's neck
to check any sound. Lung's blue coolie coat made only a
passing shadow as he stooped into the cave.

For a moment he crouched, widening his eyes in the darkness. Reflected light showed him the strange silvery bird
sleeping in the curve of the boy's arm, head tucked under
one wing. Lung thought to himself, "Quick, now!" The
pistol butt slashed at Chuck's head.

Something inside the cave exploded at the same moment
that he struck.

Lung felt wings, hard wings, beating his head. He heard
a hissing. Lung's river-pirate days were recent enough to
tell him this was a startled cormorant.

Chuck awoke with a shriek like the air rushing out of a
Miao bagpipe. He rolled into something in the darkness
and with another yelp he rolled away. The cave was like
the cavern of the thunder gods, a tempest of winds and
shouts and hissings.

He recognized the beating of Precious Grief's strong
wings and saw someone tumbling from the cave. More
shouts followed as Lung rolled into the aroused carter. The
carter, a courageous man for all his rice-bird scrawniness, had

tripped Lung and twisted his arm behind him.

"Ai-yi, I have the thief!" he shouted.

Chuck came rolling out of the cave, feeling the gashed place where the Luger had raked his skull.

"Hold him," he urged. "The man tried to kill me."

Precious Grief was still the war bird, hissing and darting his hook-bill.

The carter quickly trussed Lung with the rope that he wore around his waist for a belt. "This man must either be desperate or mad to rob travelers so poor that they sleep beside the road in caves," the carter said, lacing Lung's wrists.

"What goes down there," a voice shouted from the walls. Light from a resinous torch reddened the watchman on the wall. He clanged his ancient pike, calling, "What's all the noise? What's all the noise?"

The carter answered, "I caught a thief trying to rob this boy. Shall I bring him to your magistrate?"

"Our magistrate is old and tired and sick. Take your thief to Red Beard at the next village. He'll see justice done."

Chuck had been pulling himself together while the watch-man and the carter parleyed. He had been staring at Lung, wondering why the man had attacked him. Then it all dawned on Chuck. A scene clicked, as detailed as any artist's brush-picture. Chuck knew the designation of this evil fruit. This was Feng's man. The Buzzard had sent his emissary to seize Precious Grief.

Chuck went back into the cave and found the pistol. He offered it to the carter.

"Do you know how to use one of these?"

"No. But I know how to use one of these," said the carter hefting a long knife with a ring atop the handle that Chuck had noticed hanging from a cord around his neck.

"Good," said Chuck. "Let's guard this man closely while I tell you a story."

So while they waited for the yellow dawn to light the Szechwan plain, Chuck told his friends how the evil old man, Feng of the Buzzards, was spreading his talons for the silver cormorant. Lung also listened, but no expression showed on his brutish face.

Chuck had always heard of the Red Beards who in centuries past had raided out of Mongolia and Tibet. In some parts of China the name Red Beard is still synonymous with raider, but Chuck had never seen any of the breed.

Now here was a whole village of them. Perhaps a quarter of the people among the whitewashed houses that fenced the Tibet road had ginger hair—men, women and children. For some reason Chuck had expected only the men to be red. Except for their coloring these people looked no different from ordinary Chinese.

When Chuck asked the carter how so many strange ones came to dwell in this village the man merely clucked.

"How would I know, boy. The red-haired ones have been living here for centuries. Perhaps in the beginning it was a matter for comment. As long as I have been using the road the red ones have been taken for granted."

They had no trouble finding the magistrate. Half the village directed them to the judge's compound and then, munching on sunflower seeds, stayed to hear the case, for the Chinese have more than their share of curiosity.

The judge was truly a Red Beard, an impressive man. He wore a mandarin cap with a red button and a black silk gown with cuffs that hid all of his hand except the proud little finger with its inch-long nail. His scraggly mustache and dagger beard made him look like a figure in an ancestor portrait.

A faint motion of his hand and a gong sounded. The bustling in the courtyard subsided. In a brisk voice the magistrate ordered the carter, "Tell your story. I am listening."

The carter told his story. He showed the magistrate the pistol that Chuck had been struck with.

When the carter finished all the villagers were straining to see Chuck and his silver cormorant. Chuck wished that he were elsewhere.

The magistrate's light-colored eyes shifted to Chuck.

"Tell your story."

Chuck told what had happened. It was not easy for him to talk before the crowd. His voice seemed small, his words came slowly, but he pressed on while the magistrate weighed him with those strange chicken-blood eyes.

When Chuck had finished, the magistrate turned towards Lung who stood truculently at the opposite side of the court-yard.

"Let me hear what you have to say. I am listening."

"If you are listening," said Lung, "tell these people to take the ropes off my wrists."

The magistrate stared at Lung coldly.

"I am listening."

Watching Lung, Chuck thought the man would bite his lip through. But then Lung started talking. He told a strange tale. He denied having had the pistol. He said he had been traveling peacefully with Chuck and the carter, and the carter's son and daughter, and that he had lain down to sleep. In the night all four had attacked him and tried to take his money.

Chuck was amazed. He'd expected Lung to deny the attack in the dark but he hadn't expected Lung to make up such a story. Lung was a polished liar. It seemed to Chuck that everyone must believe Lung for he told his story so well, so plausibly.

After Lung had finished speaking the magistrate carefully drew a pair of square glasses from a sharkskin case and with even greater care placed them on his nose. Over the tops of the glasses he examined the Luger lying on the teakwood table. He looked at Lung. To a burly man who stood at his shoulder he said, "Look under that one's jacket. See if he carries a holster for this weapon."

Lung tried to back away as the magistrate's man approached but the crowd was too thick and unyielding. The magistrate's man ripped open Lung's blue coolie coat and there, ribboning his bare chest, was the strap of a shoulder-holster.

The magistrate cleared his throat.

"Tigers and deer do not stroll together, Mr. Lung. I believe you are guilty of this near crime and perhaps many other crimes you managed more successfully. A great American philosopher once said, 'An ounce of prevention is worth a pound of cure.' So I have a peculiar punishment to fit your prevention."

The magistrate's words prodded Lung into a fury. Chuck thought he was going to bull through the crowd. But two large men had slipped up beside Lung and one slapped a harsh hand over the prisoner's mouth, stopping his flood of profanity.

Without raising his voice the magistrate called to a man in the back of the crowd. "You are on your way to the mountains, friend Sui."

"On my way to Tibet," the man Sui called back cheerfully. "Can I buy you a prayer wheel for your soul?"

The magistrate's carven face almost showed a smile.

"Better than that, friend Sui," he said. "I want you to take this man back into the mountains. Put him to work. Perhaps in time he will repent. At any rate for a few years he will be too occupied to do harm."

Like all the tribesmen from the rugged highlands of Tibet, whether they be Chian or Hsifan of Nosus, the man Sui had a fine robust sense of humor. He roared with laughter and the crowd joined in. Even Chuck, for all his youth, could appreciate the neatness of the magistrate's sentence. Mr. Lung would have to behave for the mountain people had a reputation for toughness.

"I shall take this fellow and deliver him to the Nosus, Oh Magistrate," roared Sui, his big belly shaking with mirth. "The Nosus will teach him gentleness."

But Lung wanted nothing of gentleness. He had been staring at the Tibetan, at his greasy braided hair, the silver loop in his left ear, the sheepskin cap that spoke of snow-locked mountains and weary exile and Lung did not like what he saw. He made a break for it.

The compound was packed with people but so fiercely did Lung charge for the gate that he might have broken through and escaped if Sui himself had not crashed a mighty forearm against Lung's chest and caught the strong blue cotton of his jacket.

"Ho, my prize," cried Sui. "You don't seem eager to explore the trail to the Amne Machin. Ah, but you'll like it when you get there."

They took Lung out and loaded him onto a pack pony. Then Sui mounted his own piebald animal and the little caravan jingled off towards the tall peaks of Tibet. The last Chuck saw of them, Sui was still waving his arms and breaking into shouts of laughter.

After the villagers had fed the travelers a breakfast of hot dough cakes and tea, Chuck got back into the traces with the carter and they trotted on towards Chengtu. The plain became even greener and villages were as thick as buds on a flowering quince. In the early afternoon they reached the outskirts of Chengtu. The battlemented gray walls rose out of the flat plain.

"Here I leave you," said the carter, wiping the sweat from his forehead with an equally sweaty arm.

Chuck gratefully slipped the pull-ropes off his shoulders. After this, he thought, I'll never complain about poling a sampan.

The boy and the girl shyly said good-bye. Chuck lifted Precious Grief off the cart where the cormorant had been riding like an emperor. Chuck had been thinking of Lung's pistol which the magistrate had turned over to him.

"I would like to make you a present," Chuck said to the carter and he lifted the weapon from his belt.

"No, no," said the carter eagerly. "It's too much."

SUI WAS STILL WAVING HIS ARMS.

"You saved my life," said Chuck, "and I have nothing else to give you."

The man protested but it was plain he wanted the Luger. The carter knew what a weapon like that would bring in Chengtu. It would buy food for his family for months. Finally he accepted the pistol.

"You must have a present in return," he told Chuck. Slipping the cord from around his neck the carter handed Chuck his long knife. Chuck blinked with pleasure. It was a handsome thing. The handle was of red-and-blue woven cord and a rawhide sheath protected the sharp blade. Chuck accepted with perhaps not quite the proper show of protest. He and the carter were both well satisfied when they bowed their last good-bye.

Chapter Ten

THE RIM OF TIBET

THE width of the road and the mass of houses made Chuck realize that this was a far larger city than Kunming. Perhaps I should have stayed with the carter, he thought.

A stranger in a strange land . . . The people who shuffled by or rode in wheelbarrows with their legs dangling over the sides all seemed to know where they were going, but Chuck had no place to go. He had come all this way to this teaming city to look for a sick man as lost and as lonely as himself. If Chuck had had relatives in Chengtu, if he had had money, it might have been comparatively simple. Relatives have other relatives, and money has a way of finding what it wants. But Chuck had neither. His only hope was to scan faces and inquire about wounded soldiers.

Every city seems to have a river, Chuck thought, as he

came to an arching bridge. The water ran strongly. On the
city side houses rose steeply out of the river. Many seemed
to be restaurants where people could sit and dine on cool bal-
conies. Beyond the fringe of houses lay the walls of Chengtu.

The city had known many victories and some cruel de-
feats. Once, when the city was desperately besieged and
the people starving, a general had stood atop the Tibet gate
playing a Chinese harp. The besiegers, hearing the cheerful
song and the assured music, concluded that the city was still
strong and well fed. The story runs that they furled their
banners and marched away.

Chengtu was to defeat Chuck often in the days to come.
It was a secretive city. Chuck wandered down streets where
purple rose-of-China bloomed above the walls of unseen
houses. Lacquer gates, scalloped with the golden bats of long
life, barred the way to hidden courtyards.

Chuck walked the Street of the Tea Merchants whose
shelves were packed with jars of flowery porcelain. He
passed the sweet shops where great masses of taffy hung from
hooks like braided horsetails. He went past the iron shops
that sold hand-forged knives from the size of a fingernail
to the length of a man's arm. He walked through the famous
silver section where squinting boys, no older than himself,
fashioned butterflies and miniature rickshaws out of silver
spun to the fineness of thread. He went down streets where
the sign-makers carved gold characters on boards first lac-
quered with a hundred coats of paint. Everywhere he looked
for Tien but he saw no one that even resembled his father.

If he had not been driven by the dragon of time Chuck
would not have been so worried. From the moment he
reached Chengtu he had less than six weeks to find his father

and return to Kunming. If he was not back by then, Precious Grief would go to the clutching hands of Feng of the Buzzards. Even if he did get back in time it was hard to see where the Tien family would find the money to pay Feng off. Chuck felt that if he could only find Tien, his father would know what to do.

And so he wandered down the wide streets, through the section of the scroll sellers, and the chop-cutters, and the famous street of the jade merchants, looking everywhere for the jaunty figure of Tien.

"Tomorrow we will meet and everything will be all right," he told himself at the end of each day.

Every evening Chuck returned to the river. In Chengtu the nights were still hospitably warm and Chuck waded in the river while Precious Grief practiced his art of fishing. Cormorants were rare around the inland city and certainly no one had ever before seen a silver cormorant. Chuck and Precious Grief often attracted a crowd.

On one of these evenings as the sun was dusting its golden haze over the petaled roofs and the gong towers, Chuck discovered a way to eke out his dwindling money. Since the fish seemed to have fled that part of the river Chuck had been throwing bits of tile and pebbles into the stream for Precious Grief to retrieve.

The cormorant liked diving in the cool water and Chuck liked showing off his bird to the few people who gathered on the bank to watch.

"Here, see if he can get this," said a fat merchant who had joined the crowd. He threw in a copper coin.

Precious Grief dove like an arrow and came up proudly with the coin in his beak.

"You keep it," said the man, when Chuck tried to give back the money. "I like to see your bird swim." And he threw in another coin.

More people came. Chuck put Precious Grief through his paces. In between diving he sat the wet-crested bird on the wall and called, "Catch this, Little Magistrate!" And Precious Grief caught the sunflower seeds in his hooked beak. Then he called, "It's time to come home to roost, Old Goose."

And Precious Grief got himself awkwardly airborne, flapping to Chuck's shoulder. Chuck patted the bird and Precious Grief burst forth with his ribald "haw haw." It was such a ridiculous sound from a bird that the crowd roared with laughter.

Precious Grief loved every moment. Cormorants are a strange species, almost as varied in character as the men they serve. Perhaps it's because the Chinese cormorants have lived so long with man. Some birds are sulky, dull and lazy. Others are alert, cheerful, as friendly as a dog. Some have a sense of humor. Some show off like parrots.

Precious Grief had a sense of humor and he was an instinctive actor. He would have flapped and haw-hawed all night just so long as anyone was left to watch him. But when the paper lanterns cast their reflections on the river Chuck bid the crowd "Tsai chien," and taking Precious Grief on his shoulder he trudged off to find a nook to sleep.

When he counted his money he was a little surprised to see how much he and Precious Grief had collected. Enough to buy a greatly needed pair of straw sandals, and food for several days. The act had another advantage. If people started talking about the boy with the silver cormorant perhaps Tien would hear and come looking for him.

But Tien did not come. One week had passed and there were only five weeks left. The picture of Feng of the Buzzards had come back to plague the boy. Chuck had asked at all the hospitals, at all the barracks, if anyone had seen a wounded soldier named Tien. There are millions of Chinese by the name of Tien and there had been many wounded soldiers in the city. No one remembered having seen Chuck's Tien.

Chuck haunted the tea shops, passing anxious eyed among the crowded tables, for all the news of the city shuttled across those teakwood squares. But no one knew a wounded soldier named Tien. One day he passed a gate in the center of the city guarded by two giant lion-dogs. He turned and went up the ramp thinking, "This looks like an empty place. A man without a home might look for shelter here."

It was an empty place, the place of desolation that had once been a king's palace. Inside the noble gate, built wide enough to take eight horsemen riding abreast, nothing remained but flat ruins and cabbage patches, though it stood in the middle of the crowded city.

A few soldiers sat about stripped to the waist picking fleas out of their padded blue uniforms.

"What do you want?" one asked.

"I'm looking for my father, a man called Tien. He's a soldier too. He was wounded in the fighting up by the Great Wall."

"No man by that name here," the soldier said.

"May I stay for a while?" asked Chuck.

"If you don't steal anything," said the soldier grinning. Apparently it was the company joke for there was nothing here to take except the stone lions, each weighing a couple of tons, and the ancient gateway with its inscriptions of forgotten kings. But someone had sent these soldiers to guard the place and guard it they would until they were ordered somewhere else.

It was noon and one of the soldiers brought forth a copper kettle filled with thin cucumber soup.

"Bring your rice bowl," he called to Chuck. "Since you're a soldier's son we'll share with you."

After the meal was over Chuck sat under the pagoda eaves, dreaming of the palace as it once must have been. Precious Grief squatted beside him, drowsing.

Pretty soon Chuck began thinking of his father, tall and cheerful. He must be somewhere in this city, thought Chuck. Perhaps when I walk down the street he will suddenly be standing there. First, since he is a fisherman, he will notice Precious Grief. Then he will see me. He will cry, "Ai-yi! Chuck! My Chuck!" And he will lift me in his arms and hold me the way he did when I was a little boy. And I won't cry, no matter how glad I am.

With renewed hope Chuck left the old palace and went down the street. He really felt he would meet his father before he reached the circle in the center of the city. But he saw no one who even resembled Tien.

So the days passed. Two weeks now. Only four weeks left. Chuck commenced to fear that he would never find his father and he would lose Precious Grief in the bargain.

When Chuck thought along those lines he would hold the cormorant so tightly that Precious Grief would groan fondly.

Both Precious Grief and my father, thought Chuck. That would be too much to bear.

Almost every evening Chuck would follow the walls as far as the river and there he and Precious Grief would put on their little act. Chuck had thought up a few new stunts like tossing a ball or a beanbag fish. Precious Grief sometimes missed the ball but he always managed to swim out and recover it. Then, cormorant fashion, he often tried swallowing the huge thing. When Chuck fished it away from him, Precious Grief gobbled furiously. It was always good for a laugh.

The third week trickled by—only three weeks remained. Chuck awoke one morning with the feeling that he must get home quickly now. The third week had passed with no more success than the previous two. He had looked everywhere. If his father was in Chengtu he wasn't to be found easily. Perhaps he has already started back, Chuck told himself. But deep inside him was the widening fear that his father was dead.

Chuck had slept that decisive night in a roofless hut near the breach in the south wall. A rainy night had brought a pallid dawn to match his spirits. As he started along the path that skirted the crumbling battlements he thought, by road it's a hard three weeks to Kunming. I'd better start back today. If I don't then Old Feng might likely put Mother in jail and what would become of little Pung?

Carefully Chuck counted the money in his pocket. Enough to buy food and to pay for a ride part of the distance. If it were not for his haste the journey wouldn't be too bad. But he kept thinking of the sadness that would be in his mother's eyes when she saw him cross Chin Pi Lu Bridge alone, without his father. They had been such a happy family.

As he reached the populous west road Chuck noticed hurrying groups of people. Some were on foot, some rode in the creaking wheelbarrows peculiar to this section, while others wheeled by in jingling rickshaws. They all seemed in holiday spirits.

"What's happening?" Chuck asked a sweet-vendor.

"A fair," said the man. "Every summer Chengtu has its fair."

The sweet-vendor trotted on with his slung tray. Chuck sat alongside the road while Precious Grief waddled down to the willow-fanned stream.

Everyone goes to fairs, thought Chuck. If my father is still in Chengtu he might say to himself, "I need a little cheering up." It would be a sad thing, if I missed Tien for the price of a single day.

Chapter Eleven

"THE LONGEST JOURNEY STARTS WITH A SINGLE STEP"

THE fair was a nomad scattering of thatched booths flung amongst the pine groves. It ran haphazardly to the haughty walls of a Buddhist temple. People were already wandering through the fair by the thousands. Fat Chengtu merchants paraded with their plump families. Tribesmen, in turbans and jackets of many colors, strode curiously from booth to booth. Vendors ladled out refreshments —peppered noodles, seed cakes and sugar water. A phonograph shrilled like ten monkeys in a cage.

Chuck stopped to watch a candy-man spin colored-sugar figurines of mounted warriors. He passed pottery stalls and booths where they sold mulberry wine. He stopped again to watch an old man demonstrating a Tibetan wire toy that took by turns the shape of a cage, a goldfish bowl, a hat, a wheel, a dish, a dozen other things.

He passed a row of toy stalls where they sold miniature sampans and green clay dogs with lolling red tongues. He bought a dog for Pung, putting it carefully in his money pouch.

"Hi boy, when are you going to put on your show?" a voice asked. It was a merchant from Chengtu who had recognized him.

Chuck was glad to see anyone.

"I only came to look."

"There's a big pond up by the teahouse," said the man. "You ought to give a show."

With the usual frank curiosity of the Chinese several people had stopped. They followed Chuck and his sponsor toward the temple grove where a teahouse reflected in a pool. Chuck was soon giving the peculiar whistle that sent Precious Grief diving after pennies. A cheerful crowd gathered. Precious Grief was so busy diving that he scarcely had a chance to cackle his self-delight.

"That's the smartest cormorant I ever saw," said the merchant. "I'd like to buy him for my grandson."

"Oh no," said Chuck. "I couldn't sell him. He's part of my family."

The man nodded understandingly.

Suddenly Chuck was terribly hungry. Neither he nor Precious Grief had eaten that morning. Nearby at a food stall Chuck bought a large square of bean curd for Precious Grief and filled his own bowl with noodles. They went back and squatted by the pond to eat.

A priest in the blue-gray robes of a Buddhist came to Chuck where he sat by the pond.

"The temple holds many wounded soldiers. Would you care, boy, to bring your diving bird to entertain them?"

Chuck almost stopped breathing. Hope and then the fear of disappointment raced each other, and like a Mongolian horse race there was no winner.

"Have you a soldier named Tien?"

"That I don't know," said the priest. "There are many soldiers."

Chuck tossed Precious Grief a last pellet of bean curd.

"We're coming."

The outer court of the temple was draped with the wares of the scroll-merchants. Pictures of dragon-toothed landscapes and of elegant ladies leading white monkeys made a pageant of the crumbling walls. A handsome painting of a Mongolian horseman holding a steeldust stallion caught Chuck's eye. But Chuck was only half aware of all this as he padded after the priest. For the first time he felt as if he might be on his father's trail.

In the inner court, under gnarled camellia trees, lounged twenty or thirty soldiers. Some wore bandages, some leaned on crutches, all had the lank look of sick men. Quickly Chuck's hopes folded wing.

He's not here either, he thought.

In the center of the court was a lily pond. Listlessly Chuck picked a marble from his pocket and tossed it in. Eager to show off, Precious Grief haw-hawed once and dived from Chuck's shoulder. A moment later he appeared. He flopped ashore and when Chuck squeezed open his bill out popped the marble and a pollywog as well. The soldiers laughed.

Because he felt sorry for the men, Chuck put Precious

Grief through every trick the bird knew. The soldiers were an appreciative audience, applauding and calling, "Do it again, water-crow."

"Find us some gold."

"Don't let the sharks get you, little diver."

When it was over they brought Chuck tea and fed Precious Grief on peanuts and ginger. Chuck went from soldier to soldier asking if they knew a man called Tien. Most of them simply said they had not bothered much with names in the army.

The feeling of aloneness came back to Chuck.

He is dead, he thought. I'll never see my father again. We are already alone, Mother and Pung and I.

Taking Precious Grief on his shoulder, he went through the courtyards the way he had come. Going back seemed shorter.

Chuck sat on the long stone steps thinking of what he must do. He must learn the best road south. When morning came he must start swiftly on his journey. He really should start right away.

He was absently stroking Precious Grief when he noticed a man coming through the booths. Something in the man's walk gripped Chuck. His father had walked a little like that only straighter, with more of a swing.

Chuck arose so quickly that Precious Grief squawked. If only the man would raise his head, thought Chuck. The man was carrying an ax and one of those U-shaped Chinese saws. Suddenly he did raise his head and the face was the face of Tien.

The next thing Chuck knew he was running towards his

father. Chuck felt his father pick him up and hold him the way he had held him when he was a little boy.

"Eldest Son!"

Chuck looked down at his father. Tien was smiling up at him but tears stood in his eyes.

"You came all this way to find me?"

"Yes."

"Your mother and Pung?"

"They're all right."

"I see you brought the rascal."

Tien patted Precious Grief who was cackling like a gobbler.

"I couldn't have gotten along without Precious Grief. He fed us both," said Chuck. Then he asked Tien about his wound.

Tien pulled off his army cap to show a white scar jagging his shaven skull.

"My strength is returning but for a while I didn't know anybody." He put one hand on Chuck's shoulder. "How did you manage to find me?"

Then Chuck told his father how the soldier had come to Chin Pi Lu. He told about Tien tai-tai and Pung and how they had had to pawn the cormorants to Old Feng. He told him the promise they had made the old devil—if they did not pay within the next three weeks then Feng would own all the cormorants including Precious Grief.

Tien arose, straightening his thin shoulders. "We must get back to Kunming quickly."

"It's a long way and there's so little time."

"The longest journey starts with a single step," said Tien.

Chapter Twelve

THE IMPERIAL BEGGAR

TIEN wanted to say good-bye to the monks who had nursed him and to the soldiers who had been his companions.

"They didn't know who you were when I asked about you," said Chuck.

Tien smiled. "I spoke so much of the lake and my sampan that they called me the Fisherman. Names don't matter much in a place like this."

The head monk was an ancient man with teeth so rotted that they reminded Chuck of pine nuts but in spite of his afflictions he was a cheerful man.

"This is my son," Tien saluted respectfully. "He came to find me and bring me home."

"A worthy father has worthy sons." The old man squinted at the boy. Then he noticed the silver bird on Chuck's shoulder and an odd expression grew on his face—almost a look of awe.

"A silver cormorant!"

"Ai, a cormorant," said Tien carefully.

"A Rain Bird," spoke the old monk softly. He was a little like a bird himself, Chuck thought, as he bent to stare at Precious Grief. "Where did you get this one?"

"A beggar gave him to me," said Tien matter-of-factly.

"A beggar?"

"Ai, a beggar."

"In the Year of the Horse, was it not?" said the monk. "And the beggar was fleeing southward."

Tien nodded.

The old man clacked a fan from his sleeve and commenced fanning hard though the day was cool.

"Come, I will show you a picture of a bird like this."

The monk turned and hobbled into a room off the courtyard. It smelt like a crypt, moldy and sharp, and like a crypt it was piled from floor to ceiling with bones—the bones of knowledge—scrolls and rubbings containing the wisdom of China.

The ancient smiled at Chuck. "The writings of Li Ju-chen, of K'ang Yu-wei, of Ku Yen-wu, of P'u Sung-lin and many others. If you should fish for knowledge, boy, you will find it here. But now I must search for the bird scroll."

While the monk searched, a servant even more ancient than his master brought three cups and a pot of strong tea. Tien and Chuck sipped as the old scholar, clucking to himself, fingered his tattered scrolls.

"Ah, here," he muttered, "from the Hing K'ing palace. From the Dragon Hall!" He offered one end of the scroll to Tien while he backed off, reeling the mulberry paper through cagelike fingers. Unfolded before Chuck was the painting of an emperor in a pink dragon-boat. One of his numerous courtiers held a cormorant of the same silvery tones as Precious Grief. Other white cormorants dove after gemlike fish. And through it all silver rain slanted down, dripping off the rampant prow of the dragon-boat, off the ivory tips of the imperial umbrella, and glistened on the crests of the silver cormorants.

"See," the ancient said, "the Rain Birds."

Slowly his gnarled finger traced the elegant Yan pictographs. "The rain brings floods. The floods bring ruin. But the rain birds can breast any flood. China will exist as long as a single Rain Bird fishes in her waters."

With practiced ease the monk rerolled the crackling scroll. "That was the prophecy," he said. "China still has many families but your cormorant may be the last of the Hing K'ing strain. In all my many years I have seen but three such birds. Two were lost at the time of the revolt here in Szechwan province twelve years ago. The third, a fledgling . . . ?"

His voice trailed off in a question. Tien sipped his tea as if he had not heard, as if he had not really understood what the old monk was saying.

The old man came to stand beside Chuck. He raised his hand, running one finger along Precious Grief's crest, down his neck. Precious Grief blinked comfortably. He liked the old man.

"Ah so," breathed the monk. "It does not matter now. The imperial days are over. Forgotten almost. The floods, the famines, the wars still go on." The old man folded his hands under his wide cuffs and bowed to Tien. "You made a promise and you have kept it. Kept it far better than a courtier or a clap-tongued monk."

Tien straightened his thin shoulders but he didn't answer directly. He bowed with the simple dignity that Chuck remembered so well.

"We must go now, my son and I, for we have a long journey ahead. Thank you for your kindnesses. Someday perhaps I can repay you."

The old man smiled. "Lao-Tze said, 'Better never to do a kindness than to do one in hope of recompense.'"

He escorted them through the courtyard. As many soldiers as could make it hobbled along to bid Tien farewell. Some gave him presents, what slim gifts they could muster— a twist of sunflower seeds to eat along the way, a dried seahorse to ward off mountain sickness, a thimble of salt, a candle stub to light the night.

Just at the gate the old monk spoke softly to Tien, so softly that even Chuck could scarcely hear.

"The beggar is dead. He died in Rangoon. The Rain Bird is yours. Guard him well, he is part of China's fate."

Chuck saw his father nod.

Then they went down the stone steps and through the pines.

Chuck was happy as he and his father left the crouched walls of Chengtu behind. His thoughts raced ahead, across the miles, across the mountains, to where his mother and Pung waited each Saturday evening by Chin Pi Lu. Chuck imagined their surprise, their happy faces, when he came marching across the bridge beside his father.

His father's thoughts too must have been strolling in Kunming for Tien said, "Wait."

Out of his cowhide knapsack he pulled a dirty, rolled up piece of felt. He took off his army cap of flimsy India cotton and unrolled the felt. It was his old fisherman's hat, more crumpled and battered than ever. Jauntily he slapped it on his head.

"Now I am Tien the fisherman."

They strode along between bent and twisted cassia trees. Farther on the road was lined with towering chestnuts planted by kindly men so that travelers might gather food along the way.

Chuck's thoughts rambled back to Precious Grief. The monk had called his cormorant a Rain Bird, of the old imperial breed. Chuck could now understand Old Feng's determination to own Precious Grief. A bird as rare as that must be worth a fortune. He reached up and petted Precious Grief where the cormorant rode his shoulder and the bird gave him an affectionate peck in return.

"Ai," said Tien, reading Chuck's thoughts, "Precious Grief is valuable. But more than that, he's our luck. We must save him from Old Feng."

Surprisingly it was not Chuck who wearied most after the first few days. It was Tien himself. His head wound had drained his stamina and the two bowls of rice each day, which was the most the monastery could afford to feed its patients, had left him weak. Day by day Tien grew more silent. The jauntiness that Chuck loved had left his father. He hardly spoke. Every bit of strength Tien husbanded to drive himself towards Kunming.

A few days of swift walking, along roads that were ancient

when Marco Polo came, took them high into the hills. The road climbed in long steps, about twice a pony's length, so that caravans could use it.

The hills swelled into mountains where an occasional gong tower was the only building in sight. By then it seemed to Chuck they were walking in a trance. His father was a scarecrow hobbling along with weight bent to a stick. Chuck carried the knapsack with its boiling-pot and rice bowls. Precious Grief, riding his shoulder, felt like a large bronze Buddha, and even the Chengtu knife on the cord about his neck dragged him down. Yet they plodded on with the determination of men born to hardship.

One evening more than two weeks after they had started, just as they reached the wind-carved crest of a mountain, Tien fell beside the trail. Chuck was frightened. Kneeling beside his father he tried to lift Tien but it was like lifting a sack of rice. Tien's eyes were shut. His chest heaved.

"Father," shouted Chuck, yelling above the wind. "Father!"

Tien opened his eyes.

"I can't go on," he whispered.

"We're almost at the top of these mountains. The road runs downhill."

"But the highest mountains lie ahead."

There was no answering that.

"Stay still, I'll build a fire."

Chuck covered his father with their one tattered quilt. Placing Precious Grief on a gaunt thorn tree he scrambled off to gather wood.

This was a dead land. Bare rock showed like flesh through a beggar's shirt. Only a few wizened bushes and an occasional pine, leaning to the rocks, broke the monotony of mountains and sky. Nothing moved. Not even a bird gave life to the landscape.

As Chuck's knife hacked the dead branches of a pine he decided, Tomorrow I must get him down to a valley. He must rest.

He thought again of his mother and little Pung waiting by Chin Pi Lu. They would not smile for a long time if he failed to bring his father home. We'd better not hurry to Kunming, decided Chuck. Otherwise we'll never reach it.

When Chuck got back to his father with an armful of wood it seemed to him that Tien looked faintly better. Soon Chuck had a small fire going. He boiled the tea-water and he and Tien shared the last rice cake.

Even that small amount of food and warmth helped to revive Tien. He sat up.

"A good son," he said. "You'll make a good man."

For a moment Chuck forgot his hunger and the cold. Maybe things will work out after all, he thought.

Then, as if the gods suddenly remembered Tien the fisherman and his son, the sound of a plane came to Chuck. The night grew alive.

Chuck craned his neck but the fresh darkness remained like a blanket. The mutter grew into a rumble as the plane slid low over the peaks. Suddenly a red and green light blinked and the motors slowed and coughed. Chuck had seen enough planes come into Kunming to know that this one was landing.

"There's a field nearby," Chuck told his father. He added with a sudden flare of hope, "I know an American flyer. He'd help us."

Tien could not so easily be lifted from his discouragement. "We can't call him, nor could he land on a mountain top."

"No," said Chuck, "but there must be a field down below."

His father refused to be cheered. "There are many fields in China. Many planes. Many flyers."

"I'm sure if we reach the field there'll be a way of finding the redheaded American," Chuck said stubbornly.

Chapter Thirteen

S O S FOR CAPTAIN SCOTT

IN the morning Tien was a little better.
They made some tea and pushed on. Chuck was still excited
about the plane but he said no more to his father.

From the mountain top they could see the field. The runway was only a white feather on a sand bar in the middle of
a great winding river. But it was unmistakably a field for
there was the radio hut and the ever-present drums of gasoline.

Chuck seized his father's hand. "Hurry. We must get to
the airfield. I'm sure they'll help us. See, Captain Scott
gave me his own good luck piece."

Chuck took Captain Scott's identification bracelet from
where he had hidden it in the waistband of his trousers. The
silver band with its name and serial number impressed even
Tien.

"Let us try. We have nothing to lose."

It took more than half a day to descend the mountain, and several hours, following the boundaries of the rice fields, to reach the river. It took time to bargain the piratical ferryman down to a fair price.

Chuck left his father and Precious Grief as soon as they stepped ashore and ran across the crushed-rock landing strip to the control shack. Inside sat a big-bellied Szechwanese with a set of earphones dangling under his chin.

Chuck showed him Scott's identification disk and asked if the redheaded American flyer ever landed there.

"Sometimes," admitted the radio man.

"Soon?" Chuck asked anxiously.

"Who can say. This is an emergency field."

"Couldn't you find out?" pleaded Chuck. "I'm a friend of his."

The radioman eyed the ragged boy suspiciously.

"I am busy now," he said.

He was working on himself with an elegant pick set containing three prongs, each of a different shape, one for the nose, one for the nails, and one for the ears. Chuck saw he was the kind of man that has to be bothered.

"You'd better find Captain Scott," said Chuck with more assurance than he felt.

The Szechwanese eyed Chuck shrewdly. The boy looked poor and dirty but then you never could tell who an American might know, especially these crazy flyers. So he removed his army-surplus boots from the table and tuned in on Nanking.

Much chitchat followed. It was not until almost an hour later when he had gotten Sian, far to the north, that the operator contacted Captain Scott. Sian was socked in and the captain was grounded.

After considerable conversation the Szechwanese raised faint eyebrows.

"You're Tien Chuck, eh? Well, the captain says for you to sit tight and he'll be along." He added, glancing down regretfully at his own big belly, "He says for me to feed you. I hope you're not hungry."

Chuck grinned. "I'm hungry right now. My father's hungry too."

Sadness touched the operator's bland face. "And rice so costly."

Just then Tien appeared in the doorway. The lowland air had given him back some strength and put color into his cheeks. On one arm he carried a crowing Precious Grief and in the other hand he dangled a fat fish.

"Ai-yi," said the radio man, brightening immediately. "Where did you get the fish?"

"Out of the river," said Tien.

For the first time the fat Szechwanese rose to his feet. He looked odd with combat boots showing under his old-fashioned gown.

"Fish and almonds in sweet-and-sour sauce!" he intoned. He walked to another door. "Boy," he bellowed into the dark room. "Boy, fan the charcoal. We have guests for dinner and one of them has brought us the gift of a fish."

Four days they waited for further words from Captain Scott. In all that time not a single plane put down. Truly this Yangtze field was for emergencies only.

At first Chuck didn't mind the delay. He was so tired that

he slept twenty-four hours straight. Tien slept almost as long. Chuck was grateful for the rest and food that put strength into his father's step and life into his eyes.

By the third day though, Chuck had enough of eating and sitting in the sun. He began to wonder if Captain Scott would really help them. Half a week remained before the day when Precious Grief would become the legal property of cruel Old Feng. Suppose the captain did get them to Kunming in time, there was still the matter of money.

On the fourth day, precisely as the fat radioman sat down to his luncheon, which was on the dot of twelve noon, the radio began to squawk. Filling his mouth full of fried rice, the Szechwanese strolled over reluctantly. He listened for a moment and then Chuck saw him glance out towards the wind sock. He spoke some instructions and nodded to Chuck.

"Captain Scott. Coming in."

Chuck jumped up and went to the door. As yet he could not even hear the plane, but after a little while he caught the mumble of twin engines. Skirting a hump to the north a C47 quickly put on size. As Chuck watched her he said to himself, "Some day I would like to fly one of those. Some day, maybe, I'll be a pilot." It was the first time he had ever considered being anything other than what his father, his grandfather and his great grandfather had been—a fisherman.

Bounced by the valley drafts the plane sloped in like a lazy kite. Chuck watched anxiously as the pilot slowed his motors. A lot of river and not much field lay ahead. The C47's landing-gear actually rippled the water as she reached for the handkerchief runway. She touched the strip, bounced, touched again, and the brakes screeched like a thousand wind-demons. At the end of the island, almost into the river, she shuddered to a stop. Chuck thanked the worried gods who watched over flyers.

Pivoting, the C47 taxied to the tower. With a final challenge the motors died. The props were still spinning when the cargo hatch banged open. Captain Scott, his red hair whipped by the prop wash, stood in the opening. He looked bigger than ever in a hip-length flight jacket and Kalgan boots.

"Hi, pung yo," he called to Chuck. "How's business?"

Grinning shyly, Chuck trotted to meet him.

"I did not know whether you would come."

"One thing about us Texans, we always keep our word," said Captain Scott. "But you certainly have traveled a far piece from where you were the last time I saw you."

They shook hands American fashion and Chuck felt large and proud. He led the flyer to the tower to meet his father.

Tien spoke apologetically. To him it seemed unbelievable that an important foreigner should come to aid a penniless fisherman and his son.

"Think nothing of it," Captain Scott told him genially. "I'm glad to give you fellows a lift. Kick your rice bowls aboard and we'll head for Kunming."

Picking up Tien's knapsack and the quilt, Scott and the co-pilot, a cheerful Chinese called Joe, tossed the things aboard the C47.

Inside the plane were a half-dozen slightly air-sick passengers and a large amount of cargo. Captain Scott cleared some important-looking crates off two of the seats just behind the pilot's compartment and made room for the Tiens.

"Don't bother about strapping yourselves in for this take-off," Scott said cheerfully. "We either get off or we crash. No second try."

Chuck settled Precious Grief carefully in his lap. He looked across at his father but Tien didn't seem frightened. He looked happy.

He's thinking how soon we'll be seeing Mother and Pung, decided Chuck. And we still have three days from tomorrow sunup to somehow find the money to save Precious Grief.

Up front there was a ticking. Then a roar. After a minute's warm-up the C47 rumbled forward, rolling slowly towards the far end of the sand bar. From the window the Yangtze looked hungry and eager to swallow a fat plane or two.

At the end of the strip the C47 swung around. Her twin motors whined like Miao bagpipes. Then the C47 leapt ahead. Chuck had just time to glance at the radioman, lolling in the doorway of his lonely shack. The runway tilted like a dropped plate. They were over water and the shadow of wings was racing to overtake their flight.

After they had flown an hour or more Captain Scott came back and hollered in Chuck's ear, "Want to come up forward?"

Chuck nodded vigorously. Shoving Precious Grief at Tien, he followed the tall captain.

The pilot's compartment was more marvelous than Chuck had expected. Even the Thieves' Market had never displayed so many dials and gauges. The look of the terrain running below was different too. Here in the nose you could see mountains stretching out endlessly towards the horizon. The country lay like a sea below.

Captain Scott slipped behind the controls. The co-pilot

climbed out from behind his yoke and gestured to Chuck. Scott nodded so Chuck slid into the kingly seat.

The C47 droned across mountains that looked like tidal waves turned to stone. Through his excitement Chuck's mind was beating urgently, Hurry. Hurry. Hurry. After those many slow miles afoot the speed of the plane should have been wonderful. But now that he was going home time seemed to press more than ever. He thought of his mother and Pung, of their smiling, happy faces. Chuck could not wait to get back to them and the creaky old sampan. Having been counting the days he knew this was Saturday. Tien tai-tai and Pung would be waiting at Chin Pi Lu Bridge.

The sun was lowering and the raw sides of the storm-gouged mountains were burnished a dusty bronze when Captain Scott turned and wiggled a finger, pointing to distant water.

"Recognize that place?"

When Chuck shook his head the flyer pointed below to villages and dyked fields spidered towards the mass of a walled city.

"Kunming?" Chuck asked, fighting the tears that suddenly jammed his eyes.

Scott nodded. "We'll soon be there."

The co-pilot tapped Chuck on the shoulder, nodding for him to trade places. Chuck went back and strapped himself in.

He grinned across at his father. "Soon now."

Tien nodded. "Soon." He looked stronger than he had since leaving Chengtu.

Chapter Fourteen

LONG WAITING

THE Kunming airstrip was broad and quiet. The setting sun tinted the rice fields the soft gold of Fukien lacquer. Buffalo carts crawled in from the fields. Cemeteries made little lumps among their groves of trees. The Yunnan countryside was a quilt of fields and ditches and pine groves dwindling towards the lake. Even from the sky it was familiar and friendly.

Chuck, smoothing Precious Grief's feathers, thought, only two miles to the bridge. We can walk that by nightfall. It's Saturday so maybe we'll catch Mother and Pung at Chin Pi Lu. They will be trudging in but they won't really be expecting us. . . .

He was deep in homecoming visions when the plane's motors cut and the C47 slid in for a landing. She touched like a dancer, rolling along until the brakes slowed her ground rush. Chuck and his father were among the first out. They were both thinking of the old bridge at Chin Pi Lu. However they paused to thank the American and his co-pilot.

Captain Scott dismissed their gratefulness with a wave of his big hand. "Forget it," he said. "If you want to wait a few minutes Joe and I can give you a lift."

Chuck would have preferred to start right out and so would Tien but politeness held them. They followed the pilots over to the dirt-gray operations office hardly knowing what they were doing.

Up in the air it had seemed calm but here on the ground a gale was blowing. The wind sock stood out straight, pointing southwest, and the tamarisk trees tossed like pony manes. Chuck and Tien hardly noticed, but Precious Grief gave a couple of squawks and sidled up Chuck's shoulder, clutching until Chuck yelped and took him into his jacket.

Their minds were so far ahead of them in happy anticipation that they hardly noticed the henna-bearded man in the peaked Mongolian cap and the felt boots and who stood watching them from the gate. Chuck thought absently that he resembled the pack-train men along the Chengtu road.

In a few minutes Captain Scott came out of the operations office and Joe swung around the corner in a jeep.

"Hop in," said Scott. "Joe and I are headed for some chow."

Almost before Tien and Chuck were aboard, Joe shot off down the road.

As soon as he saw that the jeep was headed towards Kunming, Red Beard went into the operations office. With the calm assumption of a man who has always taken what he wanted he seized the telephone from the clerk and called a

JOE SHOT OFF DOWN THE ROAD.

number. Then in the quick Pekinese dialect he gave clipt orders to someone at the other end. When he was through he shoved the phone back at the cowed clerk and strode out quickly. It had taken but a moment.

Meanwhile Tien and Chuck were jeeping towards Kunming. This was much faster than walking but certainly not so good for the soul. Precious Grief stuck his head out to see what the trouble was and tried to balance with outstretched wings, making it very uncomfortable for Chuck. With the wind raging and the jeep bucking over the cobbled road it must have seemed like a storm on the lake to Precious Grief.

"Where can we drop you off?" called back Scott.

"We wish to stop at Chin Pi Lu Bridge," Tien said. "My wife and my younger son come on Saturdays to wait for us. We hope they will be there."

When they reached the bridge, almost deserted because of the wind and approaching rain, Tien tai-tai was not in sight nor Pung either. Tien, hiding his disappointment, thanked the flyer politely while Chuck unloaded their few belongings.

"We'll stop on the way back from the old Boiling Pot in case you want to bunk at the field. It's going to rain cats and dogs before long," Captain Scott called cheerfully as he ground off in low.

Neither Chuck nor Tien was worried about a little rain. They had come far and waited long for this moment and a flood wouldn't have budged them. In the gateway of the peeling yellow custom house they took shelter as Chuck had done other nights with his mother and Pung. Now he felt older and more successful. Waiting was a joyous agony.

But one deep worry still nagged Chuck's mind. He had been thinking and thinking but he could see no way of keeping Precious Grief out of Old Feng's claws. He had even considered asking Captain Scott to lend him the money but somehow this went against the grain. Scott had already done him great favors.

Chuck spoke about it to his father as they huddled in the wet gateway while the rain and wind tore the bark off the eucalyptus trees in the walled garden beyond.

"I do not know what we can do," Tien said sadly. "Perhaps I could borrow some money from Li, the banker, but he is almost as big a robber as Feng. Also he does not know the value of the birds."

They sat there, huddled in their single quilt, trying to see through the shiny darkness. Several times Tien got up and prowled the bridge. He found no one.

"I don't think they will come tonight," Tien said. "The storm must have been bad on the lake."

"Then they won't come for another week," Chuck said.

He sat holding Precious Grief, running a finger up and down his neck. The excitement and the joy, fled and gone, left Chuck empty.

It was perhaps midnight when a car drew up and stopped near the bridge. All Chuck could see was the rain slanting through the headlights but he recognized the jeep horn. Only Captain Scott would blare out like that in the middle of the night.

Buttoning Precious Grief into his jacket, Chuck went out into the rain. Tien sloshed beside him.

The American leaned over from behind the wheel and Chuck could see his pleasant wet grin in the reflected shine off the cobbles.

"Any luck?"

"No one has come."

"You'd better hop in. We'll find you a dry bunk at the field."

Chuck turned to look questioningly at his father. There was a sudden heavy patter as if the raindrops had increased to giant size. Chuck saw a knot of men trotting across the bridge. Something was wrong!

"Go! Go!" he yelled.

That was all he had time for. A bamboo whacked him across the forehead. As he went down he saw arms reach out to seize his father. He heard a hurricane roar from Captain Scott just as his head hit the parapet and he dimmed out.

Chuck awoke to find himself beating against the steel bottom of the jeep. He knew what elders meant now when they said they had a headache. It wasn't good. He was tight bound, arms and legs, but by turning his head he could tell that his father was beside him. Also Joe, the co-pilot, was piled in the back but Captain Scott rode in front. Always, thought Chuck with wry humor, the foreigners get the front seats.

The jeep was beyond the town Chuck could tell by the spacing of the houses and the tall trees along the road. He could smell the dank rice paddies and soon he caught the familiar freshness of the lake. Without warning the jeep jumped to a stop and Red Beard turned and scowled back at them.

"All here," he said to himself, "including that ill-fated bird."

For perhaps five minutes they waited and then the sound of trotting feet came clearly out of the night. Soon half a dozen hard-breathing men stood around the jeep.

"Get them into the boat," rasped Red Beard.

Hands reached in and grabbed Chuck. He was carried for some distance like a bedroll and then tossed briskly into the bottom of a gravelly sampan. Joe, swearing in elegant Mandarin, was tossed on top of him. A few moments later they brought Tien. After considerable time and plenty of noise Captain Scott landed in the same place. Chuck wished that he understood what the American was saying. It sounded interesting. Last of all came Precious Grief, cackling furiously.

The lake was rough. Water slapped over the sides and the oar-pins made a gritty sound as if the ropes were stretching. It did not seem to Chuck that the men were boatmen. He was relieved when finally, after some hours, the sampan bumped shore.

Though it was still black night, Red Beard had the prisoners blindfolded. Then their ankle ropes were cut and they were yanked ashore. Someone jerked the Chengtu knife from around Chuck's neck.

"West Mountain," whispered Tien. "Hear how the waves slap the big rocks?"

Chuck listened. He could hear the drum of the waves on the rock-strewn shore and he could picture the bald-faced mountain rising like a monument out of a tangle of boulders and pine thickets.

From a scabbard strapped across his back Red Beard drew a tai ping sword and pricked his prisoners up the steep trail. They came to some worn steps and climbed endlessly straight upwards. Finally they were on a soft trail again. Eventually a guard hailed them.

"It's me," called Red Beard. "Open up, man. Open up."

A gate squeaked rustily ahead. Still blindfolded, with Captain Scott still swearing away under his breath, they were pushed into a passageway. Through the cold wet material of his jacket Chuck could feel the even colder stone walls. After a hundred paces they came into a drafty chamber that smelt of punk and sandalwood.

"I've got them all," Red Beard announced, "and here's the bird."

The voice that answered was thin like a worn phonograph record, and faintly familiar to Chuck.

"Ah, so. Take off the blinders," the man said. "They won't get out of here unless they possess the strength of General Kwan."

When the bandage had been jerked down Chuck saw why the voice was so familiar. It was Feng—Old Feng of the Buzzards. He was smiling and stroking Precious Grief who cowered between his bony hands.

"So you have come back, Tien, you and the boy. You are able to pay your debt?"

"Give me time and I'll get the money," said Tien.

Captain Scott had been following the conversation with angry interest. "I don't know what Tien owes you but I'll pay if it's within shootin' distance."

"Ah yes, so complicated," said Feng, glancing at Red Beard in a half-annoyed and half-amused way. "So many willing friends but all too late."

"What do you want? What's your idea of highjacking us?" said Scott impatiently. "I'm tired of games."

There was an ugliness in Feng's one good eye, as he looked from Captain Scott, to Tien, to the co-pilot Joe, and finally to Chuck, that frightened the boy. He wished the American would guard his tongue more carefully for there was a tinder-dry danger in Old Feng.

"This is no game," said Feng. "I have always thought that people that played games were foolish. It is just that I have long wanted this silver cormorant. The tea leaves said that if I did not seize the bird as soon as he reached Kunming then I should never get him. Now I have him and I shall keep him. I do not think that you understand this because you come from a different land," he said to Captain Scott. "But perhaps Mr. Tien understands somewhat."

"He is my bird. He is my son's bird. We want him," said Tien stoutly.

Feng's fingers twitched around Precious Grief and he gave that strange laugh like breath being blown through a straw.

"I am a reasonable man so I shall explain. After all you gentlemen must pay extravagantly for my wish and I think I owe you that. You see," he continued, and his eye glowed with memory, "I was Keeper of the Falcons at the court of the last Empress. In those days the court at Peking was glorious and one of its richest treasures were the Imperial Rain Birds, the silver cormorants. They were supposed to have been sent by the gods."

Precious Grief fluttered in Feng's lap, straining to get away, but there was tenacity still in those bony hands.

"Ai, the Empress is dead, the court dead, and Feng has been like dead these many years." He laughed. "But before I go to my coffin for good I shall once more possess an Imperial Rain Bird. Only an old man's whim but all an old man has is his whims."

"You have the bird—what shall I do with *them*," Red

Beard asked impatiently.

Feng's eye moved slowly across their faces, chilling Chuck to the bottom of his empty stomach.

"Too bad," he said, "but what are three or four more people in a too crowded world. Lock them up in the round chamber. We will think of some simple way."

There was something so final in Feng's voice that Chuck could almost feel the cold night waters of the lake closing over his tightly bound body.

As Red Beard prodded them from the room with his Japanese automatic, Chuck heard Precious Grief cawing wildly. This is the end of us all, thought Chuck.

With Captain Scott in the lead they marched down another short passage and through another teak door. The room they entered, lit by two tallow dishes, was precisely circular. The floors were smooth except for ancient traceries but the damp walls still bore the marks of dull picks. The ceiling was high and irregular which seemed odd in that precise room. Two benches bisected the opposite walls. The door squeezed shut and they were locked in with their four shadows. For a few minutes no one spoke.

Then Captain Scott moved decisively. "We've got to get out of here fast. That old devil means to kill us. Look . . ." He held his lighted cigarette as high as his arm would reach. Chuck watched grimly, too miserable to care much what his friend was up to. He noticed though that the pale smoke moved eagerly upwards towards a corner of the ceiling where the rock lay in rough stratas. The smoke flowed into the same seam from which water dripped.

"Sure as shooting, there's a hole up there. You game to take a look-see, boy?"

At first Chuck did not realize what the American meant. Still numbed by the loss of Precious Grief and his own fears he glanced up dimly.

"Joe, climb on my shoulders," Scott said to the co-pilot. "We'll make a ladder against the wall for the kid to climb."

"He's gonna need jets," Joe said, smoothing his lacquer hair cheerfully. But he mounted Captain Scott's broad shoulders and, placing his hands cautiously against the damp wall, he straightened up. Someone lifted Chuck—his father's strong hands.

"Try it boy. It may lead us out of here."

Chuck managed a faint grin as he was hefted ceilingwards up the human ladder. He did not feel too secure. But then his hands hooked into a fold in the rock and he could feel the welcome draft on his face. Cautiously he peered into the dank and slimy opening that smelt of sulphur and darkness.

The cleft in the rock was wider than it looked at first. It did not go straight upwards but angled off gradually. Chuck decided that in ancient times this had been built as an escape tunnel. But men must have been smaller in those days. Neither his father nor Captain Scott could get through this.

Joe gave him a final heave. "Okay?"

"Okay," Chuck whispered. "I think I can squeeze along."

"If you work your way out of this joss house try to get an idea of where we're located. Then get the constabulary," Scott said.

Chuck started crawling. It was like going up a slanted chimney where the soot had turned to slime. Under Chuck's hands and knees was a mess of stuff that felt somehow alive. It took all his will power to keep pushing onward.

Without warning the tunnel widened and became faintly

light. He could stand up though the rock was damp and slippery. The walls, like the chamber below, had a basket-weave look, a design of blunt and patient picks.

Chuck wasted no time. Rubbing his wet hands on equally wet trousers he moved as quickly as the slime would permit. His feet found steps. Drains had been cut in each side to channel the water but the rock was still damp and mossy. A hundred steps down he saw real light. Morning sunlight.

When he reached the bottom Chuck was amazed to find he was facing another wall. The light came through a funnel in the rock. For a moment Chuck felt sunk until he saw the outline of a stone door in the wall in front of him. It was even notched for a handhold.

Chuck tugged. The rock slid towards him as if on rollers. He squeezed out. Another scarp of stones served as a screen. There lay Kunming lake—Tien Chih as it was called—a spread of pale morning silk. Above him were the Taoist shrines carved on the bald heights of West Mountain. He knew now just where he was. Directly below, walled with trees, was Smugglers' Cove.

It was wonderful to be free, to be out of that dankness and dread. But fear was still riding Chuck's shoulder. He made a quick survey so he could relocate this spot, then started downward. He scrambled through pines and over slabs and boulders. Soon a faint path among the wild azaleas caught his eye. Following it down the mountain he came to a grove of eucalyptuses. A strange, remembered smell reached him, a smell peculiar to fowls. Only then did he realize that the trail led directly to the grove where Feng kept his unhappy birds.

The knowledge that he was near Feng gave Chuck no

comfort. He remembered Feng's man who had tried to get him at Chengtu. But there was no way through the euca- lyptuses except close to Feng's cave, so he kept on down the trail.

Chuck moved through the grove as quietly as he could but dead strips of bark kept crackling underfoot. Part way through, catching a flash of movement, he froze. So slowly that it was painful, he turned his head. In the clearing out- side the cave with the scarlet curtain, sat Feng. In front of him on a table, tied by a leg, squatted Precious Grief.

Chapter Fifteen

A TRAP FOR THE UNWARY

WITH one old claw Feng held the bird by the shag and with the other he massaged the base of Precious Grief's neck way down by the wishbone.

Chuck watched, shivering a little at the fear that Feng of the Buzzards always aroused in him. Red Beard, he thought, would kill quick, but Feng would kill more cruelly.

No time to waste. Chuck slipped out of his sandals, knotted them and slipped them around his neck. He moved from tree to tree with a stealth he hadn't known was in him. Along the path he spotted two guards boiling their breakfast rice. Down by the cove he saw several more of Feng's bandits splashing water over their shaven heads. Rifles were stacked nearby.

Chuck found a path that followed the lake margin. Ahead, perhaps two miles away, he could see the ferny tops of ginkgo trees that shaded the Kunming road. Further along was the customs' station. There would be police there.

Chuck trotted as fast as his boy legs would allow. The rocks cast down by West Mountain gave way to fields. The path became a shaggy road that curved by farms and a village. Out in the lake Chuck could see the sails of sampans and junks quartering on a faint breeze towards Kunming a few miles across the lake. He wondered if one of those craft held his mother and Pung.

Nothing had changed on the Burma Road. Farmers passed carrying pigs trussed to poles. Pony carts rattled along, and every so often a coke-burning truck chugged by as if on its last dilapidated journey.

As he spotted the tower of the customs' station Chuck's pace increased. His troubles were almost over now. Help was in sight. He was ready to weep with relief. The guard looked at him indifferently and let him pass. Inside the station a dozen more lazy guards were tying up their sleeping mats on the long customs' counters.

"The officer?" Chuck asked a lad not much older than himself. The boy wagged his head towards a room at the far end of the hall.

Chuck approached the door and paused. He could hear a rumble of voices, a deep bellowing laugh. The laugh was familiar. Chuck moved closer and glanced through the partly opened doorway. Two police lieutenants, tunics still unbuttoned, sat on their cots. With his back to the door stood a bulky figure in a padded coat and Mongol boots.

Red Beard! He started to turn . . .

Chuck turned and ran. He scurried from the building like a chicken chased by a hungry dog. Only faintly was he aware of the half-curious, half-indifferent glances of the men. The guard at the door brought his machine-pistol to the ready but no one seemed to be after the boy so he let him pass.

Chuck just ran, not noticing where he was going. I must get away from Red Beard, he thought. I must get away before he gets me. Feng and his men seemed everywhere. Red Beard obviously was a friend of the police.

Chuck took the first side path not caring where it led. Get away! Get away! Get away! He ran on, taking a razor-edged footpath that served as a rice field boundary. Under a willow he paused to get his breath.

This moment held the greatest quandary of his life. The fate of his father, Captain Scott, the co-pilot and Precious Grief hung upon the whim of Feng. Where there should have been help there was no help. It needed the wisdom of Confucius. But there was no one here to solve the problem but Chuck the boat boy.

From where he squatted under the praying willow Chuck stared out at the lake. Even now, for all his despair, he knew a faint feeling of comfort in being home. From the time he had been a child the lake had always answered his questions. Perhaps it would answer him once more.

Chuck watched for sails but they were far off and there were none he recognized. He stared at the Temple of the Western Cloud. Close by in a hidden crypt, somewhere within the mountain, his father waited. Chuck wondered if any but Feng's band knew of that secret place.

His eyes came to rest on a wooded point perhaps three miles across the water. There, that stormy day, the sampan had been wrecked. There lay the village of Scarface the smuggler. Scarface who hated Feng so ferociously.

Chuck jumped up. The lake had answered him again. If the police could not be trusted he would put his faith in the smuggler.

Three miles was all it was to Scarface's hideout by water but by land it was three times the distance. The sun was past its zenith when Chuck trotted across jig-saw slabs that bridged the creek separating Scarface's island from the mainland. He paused under a tamarack as a man stepped into the path. The man carried a mattock but he carried it more like a weapon than like a tool.

"What do you want, boy?" he asked, planting himself in front of Chuck.

"I want to speak with your chief," Chuck panted. He had come a long way fast and he knew now what it meant to stand on your last legs.

"He's not here."

"Where is he then? I must see him."

"A popular man, our chief," said the farmer. "People come from all over Yunnan just to speak with him."

"Please, please," said Chuck. "I've been here before. He knows me. It's important."

A voice spoke up from the nearby paddy. "Let him in, you maotai-drinker. It's the sampan boy." And the man who had been secretly watching from the reeds stood up, cradling a brass-bound fowling piece in his arms.

"Ah, so. Ah, so," grumbled the other. "You know everything, Sharp Eyes. All right, come along boy."

He led Chuck through the patch of woods to the village where the houses turned inward. Chuck was met by the same guarded stares that he remembered from before. He was taken to Scarface's house. The same old lady dozed under the broken tiles. The same pig, scarcely a pound fatter, nosed in the muck. Scarface's wife remembered Chuck.

"What's the matter now, boy?" she asked with peculiar patience.

"I need help," said Chuck, flopping to the ground. He was exhausted. He could not tell which hurt the most, his chest or his aching legs. He repeated grimly, "I need help."

Apparently it did not strike Scarface's wife as strange that someone should seek help of a smuggler. She glanced obliquely at the girl who stood chewing her braids and giggling. "Fetch Ho."

When the child had run off the woman brought Chuck boiled water and heated a bowl of mushroom soup. Without speaking further they both sat waiting for Scarface.

His approach was, as usual, swift and silent. One minute there was just the wife, the old woman, and the pig. The next moment Scarface stood there. He carried a hoe, and his torso was gray and black with mud from the fields. Ho was really a farmer, it seemed, as well as a smuggler.

"Well boy . . ."

The scarred face was more sardonic even than Chuck remembered.

"I came for help," said Chuck, putting aside his bowl. He told his story wondering if Scarface would believe him. There was no more expression on the smuggler's face than you would find on a stone elephant's.

When Chuck had finished Scarface continued to stare.

"It would seem our friend Feng has gambled unwisely this time. Kidnapping a pair of CNAC pilots—the governor will have to show a hand in this."

"Will you help me?" asked Chuck eagerly.

Scarface surprised him. "We'll go tonight, my men and I. I'll send word to the governor too."

"And me?"

Scarface chuckled drily. "You too, boy."

Chapter Sixteen

THE RAID

WHEN the evening star shone through the peacock twilight, they set sail in three swift sampans. Scarface had gathered nineteen armed men. Each of the sampans carried a triangular pennant bearing a white cormorant.

"I've been a smuggler and a bandit and I've never had a flag," Scarface told Chuck as they stood in the prow of the lead sampan. "For once I fight in an honest cause. And also the pennants will keep us from firing on each other," he added practically.

When they were well into the lake Chuck asked a question he had been keeping a long time.

"Have you seen my mother's sampan?"

"Not for a month," Scarface said. "My men have seen nothing of your boat."

They sailed on in silence with only the slapping of the rattan sail and the lake gurgling softly under the keel. Chuck wondered about Tien tai-tai and Pung. It was another worry added to his pyramid of fears.

Less than an hour later they stood a mile off Smugglers' Cove. Scarface rattled down his sail and the other sampans dropped theirs so swiftly they seemed like echoes. The three boats touched.

Scarface gave brief orders. He curved his arms like horns showing how the sampans would land, one on each side of Feng's stronghold. He pointed to where his own boat would go in some distance up the shore from the eucalyptus grove.

"Don't stir until you hear shots. Then close in fast."

The sampans drifted apart. Oars where slid out. The boats moved softly across the dreaming lake. Only a sickle moon and a few stars lit the sky and sometimes these were cloud covered.

Off a point about a mile from Feng's cave they anchored the sampan and waded ashore. Scarface and his men had an odd assortment of weapons—several U.S. 30 caliber carbines, a couple of Chinese fowling pieces, and the old carpenter carried an ivory-scrolled Yunnanese cross-bow that looked the most deadly weapon of all. Scarface plucked the white cormorant pennant from the prow of the sampan and handed it to Chuck.

"Carry this boy. Keep close to my heels," he said. "I've been waiting a long time for New Year's."

At first Chuck didn't get his meaning. Then he remembered that all debts are supposed to be repaid at New Year's time. Scarface was speaking of revenge.

They had no difficulty in finding the lake path. Only the one trail led along the base of the cliffs. Chuck cautiously led the way followed by Scarface and his band. At night things look different and Chuck was worried that he might go too far and blunder into Feng's sentinels.

The smell was what warned him. One moment he didn't know exactly where he was. The next moment the bird smell struck him like a gong. Then he knew exactly where he was. He held up his hand.

Scarface eased alongside, carbine ready. "Where now, boy?"

"Up," Chuck pointed.

Up the hill was the back entrance to the crypt. But where? thought Chuck. Where? Now in the faint light of the fledgling moon the mountainside was as hard to read as a soaked newspaper. It was as full of wrinkles as a village elder's neck. Chuck had the haunting fear that he might wander for hours—wander all night—without finding the entrance. He hated to think what would happen to his father and Captain Scott. He hated to think what Scarface would do to him.

"Follow me," said Chuck with more conviction than he felt.

They moved off the path, in among the embracing boulders. It couldn't be far away, Chuck knew. In the daylight he had edged towards the eucalyptus grove for cover. Somewhere almost straight upwards was the stone that hid the entrance. He remembered that the rock had been shaped a little like a loaf of Annamite bread.

They climbed quickly, keeping low. Every fifty steps Chuck raised his head to get his bearings. For this I need the eyes of an owl and the sense of a homing pigeon, he thought despairingly.

Then suddenly, when he was about to turn back, there was the loaf slanting outward.

"Here," said Chuck more loudly than he had intended. "Now if we can open it."

"Stand back, boy. I'll open it," growled Scarface. Tossing Chuck the coil of rope he was carrying, he knelt and began to feel around the base of the rock.

Chuck never knew how the smuggler did it but the rock slid outward almost at his touch.

Scarface left three of his band, in command of the old carpenter, to guard the rear. The other two, he gestured to follow. They were small, Chuck noticed. One was old, gnarled by the years, almost a dwarf, and one was little more than a boy.

As the stone door closed behind them Scarface struck a match and lit a paper lantern. They moved quickly through the passageway, up the slimy steps. A bat, disturbed by the light, brushed Chuck's cheek and Chuck almost dropped the carbine he had exchanged for the pennant.

"Get on," Scarface snapped. "Get on."

When they came to the place where the tunnel became a badger hole Scarface nodded Chuck ahead.

"Can you follow?" Chuck asked anxiously.

"I've crawled through keyholes," Scarface said succinctly.

Skidding along on his belly through the slime, Chuck listened for voices. He could hear nothing but a faint drip . . . drip . . .

"Hurry, *pung yo*," hissed Scarface.

The passage seemed shorter coming than it had going. Chuck was soon at the spot where the tunnel funneled downward into the crypt. He felt light coming up but he could still hear no voices.

He whispered back, "How do I get down?"

"The rope," said Scarface.

Chuck slid it under his shoulder. He could just turn his head enough to see Scarface knotting the long line about his own waist, then shoving it back to the next in line.

"Slide," ordered Scarface.

Gritting his teeth against the brutal jerk he knew was coming, Chuck slid slowly over the lip. He had a glimpse of hard gray stone floor coming up to hit him. Suddenly he was jerked upright, caught by the rope that scissored his chest. Pain wrung a cry from him. Then he was being lowered like a crab into a pot.

The stone floor stunned him when he hit. A moment later he was roughly lifted and the ropes were stripped from his aching chest. Blinking the tears out of his eyes he stared around anxiously. The first thing he saw beyond the flame of a cigarette lighter was Captain Scott's grin. Then he found his father's anxious face.

"Chuck!" was all his father said but there was a world of relief in his voice.

"The kid made it," said Captain Scott. "I'd have bet my bottom dollar on him."

A moment later Scarface swung down, riding two carbines like an anchor. Then came the wizened oldster and finally the boy.

Scarface looked around briefly. Without a word he walked

over to the teak door. Tapping it lightly, he turned to the old man who followed at his heels.

"Tools!"

Out of a satin bag the dwarf selected a drill and a saw, the tiniest tools that Chuck had ever seen. Scarface started to work.

"What goes on in there?" boomed a voice.

Everyone in that shadow-flung room stopped still. Then, like a horse frightened by thunder, Scarface jumped back against the wall. The old man picked up his rifle and stepped into the shadows. Chuck ducked down.

The door swung inward and Red Beard stood there, broad as a war god, switching his sword. Two drowsy guards shuffled at his back.

"What goes on here? What do I smell? Mischief's brewing, eh?"

They were all huddled in a group like plotters, Tien and Captain Scott and Joe the co-pilot.

It was almost like a pantomime. Some campfire sense caused Red Beard to turn. He was in time to see his two guards go down. One fell from Scarface's rabbit-punch, one from a butt-blow by the dwarf.

"You devil!" snarled Red Beard and slashed at Scarface.

Chuck, watching from the side, had seen it coming. He flung the carbine to his shoulder and jerked the trigger. The gun-thunder in that closed place was like an undersea explosion. Red Beard reeled back.

Tien and Scott moved fast. Chuck had never realized how nimble his father was. One moment Red Beard was standing, sword rearing for another slash at Scarface, next his arms were caught from behind and pushed upward much the way crabs are pegged for market. Red Beard's sword dropped with a surging clang.

"The rope," gritted Scott.

Like all boatmen Tien was handy with a line. He had Red Beard helplessly trussed before the big bandit knew what had happened.

"You shouldn't have shot, boy," growled Scarface. "Give the American your gun."

Chuck had expected to be praised for his fast thinking but he meekly handed Captain Scott the carbine.

Scott grinned. "It's okay, kid. We're in the catbird seat now. They won't be able to stop us. We'll get straightened out fast with Old Feng."

They locked up Red Beard. Then with Scarface and Captain Scott in the lead they broke into the passage, through the room that Feng had used for interrogation, and on through a hidden door that came out behind a statue of Kuan Yin, the Goddess of Mercy. Just before they left the crypt Chuck had picked up Red Beard's sword. It was a weapon to give a boy the courage of a Fukien tiger.

Chapter Seventeen

DISAPPEARANCE

T HE path curled steeply downward among the wild azaleas. From Smugglers' Cove there were spurts of frantic firing, shouts, then sudden silences. Lights began to bob along the lake road and a bugle croaked hoarsely.

In the lead, Scarface had seized a handy tree trunk to stop himself. "Wait," he shouted. "Wait. Those must be the governor's troops. The fighting will swing this way. They'll drive Feng's men up the mountain."

Like a guerrilla leader, Scarface deployed his small force, placing them above the trail where it cut through a clearing. He sent the dwarf to bring up the remainder of the band that waited at the tunnel exit. Chuck found himself crouched behind a boulder with Red Beard's sword for a sharp companion.

Below, it sounded like New Year's. Torches wavered through the trees. Hoarse shouts of panicked men flung upward. With a spendthrift disregard of ammunition the governor's troops had gone into action. To himself Chuck thought, I shall have a wonderful tale to tell Pung and the other boys. He was glad though, secretly, to be seeing the battle from part way up the mountain.

Then Feng's men began to come, a rabble, fleeing up the mountainside—the one way of escape. The scud had cleared from the thin moon and Chuck could clearly see the trail. The first man who came was a bandy-legged ruffian in a padded blue army blouse. He must have had mountain blood for he climbed like a goat.

Scarface raised up, rifle in hand, calling, "Halt, and surrender."

The man stopped. He crouched. With a swift motion he tipped up his rifle and snapped a shot at Scarface. Deliberately Scarface raised his carbine and fired.

Even as the man went down, a couple more of Feng's bandits scrambled up the trail. Shots beat the bushes and ricochetted overhead. Chuck jumped as a bullet-clipped twig flipped his back.

More of Feng's men were pouring into the clearing, climbing rapidly. Chuck had not realized how large a force Feng had kept hidden there in that dim grove under the mountain. Or perhaps Feng's wary nose had scented trouble and he had called in his followers from the mountain trails where they plied their arts of banditry.

Scarface and Scott and Tien were firing carefully from behind rocks. Chuck had never seen his father so calm. Tien might have been out on the lake on a sunny day netting carp.

But Chuck knew they couldn't stop the bandits for long now. More than a score of Feng's men were working up the trail and their bullets were beating ahead of them.

Chuck called a warning to his father and began to shift back. As he slid around a pine, he ran into a man who was scrambling in from the flank. Raising up, the man swung his weapon. Chuck ducked with a yelp. He flung up his sword. Wood clanged against steel.

"Wait!" someone shouted. "It's the cormorant boy."

It was Scarface's old carpenter, the man of many trades. Chuck opened his eyes, which he had unwisely shut, and saw that the old fellow had come up with his men. One carried the cormorant pennant.

The oldster handed Chuck the flag. "Come on, you glue-pots," he cackled back over his shoulder.

A dozen of Feng's men were circling the rocks which Scarface and Tien and Captain Scott were using as a fort. Rifles cr-a-a-ng'd as the bandits drove forward. Lead ricochetted, whining off up the mountain. One of Feng's men had lit a resined bush and flung it into the trail. The flame illuminated the wild picture.

Chuck spotted his father. Tien was crouched amid the rocks, firing calmly. Captain Scott, triggering the .30 caliber carbine, was like a berserk water buffalo. Below the rocks, in plain sight, Scarface was lashing out at two of Feng's bandits with nothing but his empty carbine for a club. In a moment the smuggler would be finished.

Something streaked by Chuck's ear. He heard a buzzing, the sound a swarm of bees might have made on a summer evening. As if by magic the rifleman fell. His rifle stabbed the ground, exploding, and the man dropped across it. Chuck turned to see the ancient crossbow vibrating in the old carpenter's hands.

They lifted a shout and pressed forward. Caught in the flank, Feng's men turned and showed their teeth. But not for long. They knew that they would soon be pressed from below. Some were wounded. Some were dead. Crying retreat, the remainder turned and stumbled into the brush.

The bandits were none too quick. The remainder of Scarface's band, reinforced by soldiers wearing the black uniforms and French steel helmets of the governor's guard, came up from below.

Chuck had scrambled across to his father who had slumped down beside the rocks.

"Are you hurt?" Chuck asked anxiously.

A light danced in Tien's eyes. "I don't know. I don't care. It was worth it, boy."

Chuck knelt in the pale moonlight and ran his hands over his father's chest where there was a dark spot. A spent bullet, or perhaps a rock fragment, had sliced through Tien's thin army tunic.

"It's nothing, boy," said Tien, grinning. "How many men did you kill with that sword?"

Before Chuck could answer, Scarface hailed them. In spite of the mauling he had taken he was still as full of strut as a fighting cock. His coolie jacket, torn to strips, gave him a frenzied look.

"Feng has escaped," he called furiously. "Or he's in hiding. Follow me." And he plunged down the trail.

Some of the soldiers followed the bandits up the mountain. From above came the crash of brush, shouts, and eruptions of rifle fire. But the storm had gone by, leaving

SOMETHING STREAKED BY CHUCK'S EAR.

the clearing oddly quiet. It was as if the gods had come back
to claim West Mountain, as if they had wiped out all but the
echoes of violence with a flutter of their fans.

Scarface had gone ahead. Chuck, with Tien leaning lightly
on his shoulders, followed Captain Scott down the trail while
the old carpenter, sniffing like a Pekinese, followed behind
with his crossbow tilted under his arm. Scott had three rifles
and a couple of bandoleers slung across his shoulder.

"You never can tell when a good shootin' iron will come in
handy," he said cheerfully. As he went down the trail he
wailed, "Pistol-packin' Mama, lay that pistol down . . ."
Chuck, not understanding the words, imagined it might be an
American dirge.

Chapter Eighteen

THE GILDED COFFIN

BELOW, in the eucalyptus grove, a score of torches were whipping around in a Lolo dance—or so it seemed to Chuck as he paused on the trail above. Then he realized that this torch dance was simply men rushing around looting. Everyone was looting, Scarface's men and the soldiers alike. Working in groups of two or three they were carrying off everything movable, the Chang Kuo-lao hanging, teak chairs, the teatable, china, Oman rugs, pots and pans, robes and shoes and charcoal braziers, and even a copper-bound cask in which Feng had kept swill to feed his birds. Only the coffin remained where it stood in the center of Feng's cave-dwelling. It was too heavy to move.

"Did you find Feng?" Scarface demanded of the dapper captain in charge of the soldiers.

"The old fox must have slipped away."

"Slipped away!" snapped Scarface. Snatching a torch from the captain's hand, he stalked into the cave. For some time, ever since the worst of the fighting was over, Chuck had been wondering about Precious Grief. Having seen him last in Feng's hands, Chuck decided to follow Scarface. If anyone could find Feng it would be someone who knew Feng's tricks.

Scarface tapped the walls. He cleared the rushes off the floor so he could search the stone beneath. He found nothing.

Scarface and Chuck, followed by the old carpenter, lit fresh torches and went searching through the grove. A few of Scarface's men had maintained their posts around Smugglers' Cove. These he questioned carefully. They had seen nothing.

"The old devil couldn't have gone up the mountain or we'd have netted him," Scarface growled.

"He's hiding. I know he's hiding," the old carpenter said. "A man as tricky as Feng would have a back door to his compound."

"If you know so much, where is this door?"

The carpenter shrugged.

Scarface and Chuck kept searching. After an hour, weary and beaten and with their feet cut from scrambling through the shale, they returned to the cave where Tien and Scott and the captain of the soldiers were waiting. The only thing anyone had found was a parrot who swore at them in eloquent Mandarin.

Tien was trying casually to tip the coffin but it was as heavy as it was huge.

"Three men the size of Feng could fit into this one," said Tien.

Scarface grinned sardonically, "Perhaps it was built for Feng's whole family. I hope so."

Chuck stood hopelessly. The excitement of the battle had worn off and he had begun to feel that Precious Grief was gone forever. He and Pung would miss the foolish bird.

At that moment Chuck realized he had been hearing a sound so faint and so familiar that it had made little impression. His eyes had been looking for a hooked beak, a curved neck, and feathers of vigorous white. His ears had not been searching at all. But it was his ears that discovered that faint persistent cackling. In a flash he knew that Precious Grief was nearby.

Chuck shouted at his father. "Hear it?"

"Hear what?" asked Tien.

"Precious Grief."

Everyone stood listening. After a moment Tien shook his shaven head. "I hear nothing."

Neither did Chuck any more. Had it been his imagination? He clasped his hands around the sharkskin grip of the big sword.

Again the sound came. Chuck's face lifted to meet the confirming smile on Tien's face.

"I hear."

Scarface was again the hunter. "Where does the sound come from?"

They eyed the sooty ceiling and the bare stone walls. It was the old carpenter who spoke, pulling at his chin whisker.

"The sound comes from beneath this coffin."

Everyone stared at the magnificent coffin.

"Help me move it," said the carpenter.

Several of Scarface's band had paused outside to pack their

loot. They joined their strength to the group that was trying to lift the coffin but it wouldn't budge.

"The old boy sure believed that coffins are here to stay," said Captain Scott.

"The coffin is attached to something below," the carpenter said. He waved all of them aside.

Squatting, he ran a saw-scarred finger along the bottom where the gold filigree rippled the lustrous black lacquer base. Halfway around, the carpenter stopped. Watching his face, Chuck saw the chin whiskers quiver.

"Now try," said the old carpenter.

Scarface, always quick, jumped to the task. At his touch, the coffin swiveled. Scarface almost tumbled into the pit beneath.

Chuck was close enough to spot Precious Grief—to see Feng of the Buzzards crouched there holding the cormorant by wings and beak. He was close enough to see the surprise and fear in the old man's one good eye as he stared up at Scarface.

"You . . ." Feng said, "I killed you!"

"You killed me," said Scarface, glaring down. "And now I kill you."

A knife was in his fist. . . .

But even before Scarface could strike, Chuck saw the ancient's face contract into a knot of pain. He saw Feng's good eye grow dim. Chuck knew that Feng had died. Died of fear—Old Feng of the Buzzards who had once been Keeper of the Falcons at the vermilion court. Feng who had been an exile, a usurer, a man of many evils, had gone to a frightened death beneath his own coffin.

Chuck remembered one of his father's favorite proverbs, "After the sowing comes the harvest." For the first time he realized how true it was.

Blinded by the long darkness of the vault, Precious Grief flapped gropingly until Chuck called to him. Then with a joyous trumpeting he came flapping to Chuck, landing ungracefully on his shoulder. Reaching up, Chuck cuddled Precious Grief's sleek head against his cheek.

There were other things in the hole beneath the coffin. At Feng's feet were stacks of money and bars of gold. Jade and gold jewelry lay in a clutter. Feng had been a collector of all things valuable.

Inside the cave dwelling the atmosphere had become tense. Scarface's men and the soldiers were eying each other over ready rifles. Even the captain had lost his foppishness. He was watching Scarface with a hungry sort of calculation. Scarface was grinning tauntingly.

"Let us go," Tien said, putting his arm around Chuck.

With Precious Grief hugged close, Chuck and his father walked towards the lake. Under their feet eucalyptus bark crackled like broken porcelain, and the night was full of the piercing smell of the trees.

Chuck said regretfully, "That was an awful lot of gold."

"But not our gold," said Tien. Through the dappled trees they could see the lake stretching into the peaceful distance. "A fisherman's life isn't a fat one," said Tien, "but our troubles are simple. If a man is careful he can guide his own life. Those back there—they can't tell what monster will rise in their nets."

They sat on the shore of Smugglers' Cove, leaning against

some rocks. Soon they fell asleep. Just before he dropped off Chuck thought, still two days to go—if we needed the time. But Precious Grief was safe now. Chuck gave the bird an easy hug.

Chapter Nineteen

SCARFACE SAYS GOOD-BYE

So it came about that Tien and Chuck returned to Chin Pi Lu Bridge.

They returned on a Tuesday. It seemed foolish to Chuck for he knew that Saturday was the only day that his mother and Pung ever went there. It was Scarface's idea. Tien and Chuck and Captain Scott had rested a day and a night in Scarface's village. He had feasted them well on roast pig, pea pods, lotus strips and many delicacies. Then on Tuesday morning he had come to Tien and said in that abrupt, un-Chinese way of his, "You should leave now. I will take you to Chin Pi Lu Bridge." It did Tien no good to explain that Tien tai-tai would not be there until the end of the week.

Scarface had made ready his largest sampan and when Tien and Chuck and Captain Scott stepped aboard Scarface followed them.

"I think I'll go with you," he said with the glimmer of an ugly but not unpleasing smile. "It's been a long time since it was safe for me to wander into Kunming."

To Chuck it seemed odd to sit in the cabin with Precious Grief in his lap and be rowed by other men. He grinned across at his father and he could tell that Tien was thinking the same thing.

The sun was warm. The sky was the blue of Kwantung pottery. The water sang as they slid across the lake. There was breeze enough to fill the sail but Scarface seemed in no hurry.

As they swung around the point of willows into the canal, Captain Scott asked Scarface a question.

"When you found old Feng he said something that sounded mighty odd. He said, 'I killed you.' What did the old devil mean?"

Scarface sucked on his water pipe. He was silent for so long that Chuck thought he didn't mean to answer. Finally he spoke.

"I'm a smuggler," he said. "My father was a smuggler and so was my grandfather. When I was ten years old I commenced learning the Burma trails."

He paused for a moment, looking back at West Mountain, the first step to Burma, to Assam and India. Scarface was thinking of those days on the trail.

"I went to work for Feng for he was the spider that sat in the web. But even a smuggler needs some conscience. Feng's business was mainly slavery and opium. I didn't like it so I quit. Feng's men came after me. They took me to the mountains and sold me to the Lolos. The Lolos still use slaves. They use them worse than we use ponies, and you Americans—" he scowled at Scott—"think we treat our animals cruelly."

It was a long speech for Scarface. For a while Chuck thought he meant to say no more. Finally he put aside his pipe and went on.

"I got away from the Lolos. Feng found out about it. He decided I'd better die since I knew so much. His men had failed him once so he did the job himself."

Scarface touched his cheek. "He used a steel rod. But we who are born in the Yunnan mountains are tough." Scarface smiled again, that masklike smile. "Feng was sure he'd killed me—but I lived."

No one spoke for a while. Then Captain Scott said an odd thing. He said, "I understand much better about you now."

At the little harbor beside the Burma Road they tied up for lunch. It was another feast—steamed eggs with rice, fried lettuce and sugared water chestnuts. Dusk lay over the walled city by the time they had poled through the cypress-lined canal that meets Kunming's guardian river. Lights danced across Chin Pi Lu Bridge.

Scarface moored the sampan by the worn steps leading to the hay-market. Nothing had changed since Chuck had left. The smell of roasting chestnuts still drifted from the stall next to the bridge. Only his mother and Pung were missing from the picture.

Captain Scott stepped ashore first. Then Tien. Then Chuck, clutching the sword, with Precious Grief perched on his shoulder. Finally Scarface leapt catlike to the quay. He held a red lacquer box. He handed it to Tien.

Tien held it cautiously in his fisherman's hands. "What is this?"

"Open it," said Scarface.

A pomegranate-shaped pull lifted the lid. Even at night the bracelets and pins glittered richly.

"A gift," Scarface said blandly. "There may be times when a fisherman could use a bit of gold."

Tien bowed and held out the box to Scarface. "I can't accept this. There is nothing I can give in return."

"This is no present. This is just your share in a certain business deal," said Scarface with a smile in his secretive eyes. Remembering the gold and the jade that had lain with Old Feng under the coffin, Chuck knew what the business had been.

"Take it, Tien," said Captain Scott. "This lil ole country boy got away with plenty. I was there."

Chuck was relieved when his father put aside formality and accepted the gold. It meant that the Tien family would not have to worry for a while if the fishing was not good.

Chapter Twenty

THE BRIDGE OF CHIN PI LU

CAPTAIN SCOTT and Scarface accompanied Tien and Chuck to the bridge. Tien tai-tai and Pung were not there but then Chuck had not really expected them. He knew Scarface's sudden quirks.

Captain Scott shook hands in the American way. "Goodbye, Tien, and good luck," he said. Then he grinned down at Chuck from his bold height. "So-long, pung yo." He ran his knuckles fondly over Chuck's bristly head. "We'll meet again, you and I, somewhere along the line."

Smiling he turned and started down the moonlit road that led eastward towards the old bell tower and the airfield.

Scarface said, "I have men out hunting for your cormorants. You should find them at my village in a few days but you may not find me there." He started off but turned back as if he had forgotten something. "Wait for an hour or so."

Then he slid into the darkness with a smuggler's unconscious ease.

"A strange man," said Tien.

Chuck yawned. He was bone-tired from the night before. "Do you think he has found Mother and Pung?"

Tien gave his old wry grin. "Does the swallow know the wild goose's course?"

So they waited. They waited while the Himalaya winds swept across the Yunnan plateau and beat at the ancient city. The wind cut through Chuck's jacket and through Tien's padded tunic.

"Let's get out of this," said Chuck forlornly.

Tien put an arm around Chuck's shoulder, lending him some of his own warmth, while Chuck led the way across the bridge to the custom-house gateway. He had so often dreamed of this meeting at Chin Pi Lu. He had pictured his mother's hungry eyes and Pung's jolly little face. But here I am, he thought, cold and tired and tonight is not the night. The dream had not been like this.

When they had found the more protected side of the doorway, Tien took off his tunic and made a tent of it for Chuck and Precious Grief.

"You'll be cold," Chuck objected.

"Just being home will keep me warm," said Tien. "Now go to sleep, boy."

Chuck glanced out. Tien was hunched over, holding his elbows, watching the bridge. Chuck saw he was smiling. He won't be too cold, thought Chuck, and huddled under the coat.

Chuck never knew exactly how he awoke. The night held the high quietness of midnight. The wind had died, and

Precious Grief was hissing to himself. Chuck missed his father's shoulder. He saw him standing in the street and heard him saying, "Quick. Quick! Look boy, I think they're coming!"

Chuck blinked his sleep-bleared eyes and tried to stare down the street grown skimmed-milk pale in the moonlight. And there, lonely as night-sailing sampans, came two figures, a woman and a boy. The slip-slap of their sandals preceded them. The two came on tiredly, and yet Chuck could see their eagerness. He forgot he had ever been cold or tired.

Tien strode out to meet his wife and Pung. Tien tai-tai saw him. She stopped. Then she commenced running. Little Pung came after her bleating like a fat-tail lamb. They met in the middle of Chin Pi Lu Bridge. Chuck saw his mother was weeping. His father's face was twisted as if he were half laughing and half crying.

"Me too," shrilled little Pung. "Me too!"

He threw himself at his father and Tien lifted him high. Chuck reached up and put his arms around his mother's neck.

"You brought him back," said Tien tai-tai and she hugged Chuck so hard that it hurt.

"Ai," Chuck said. That was all he could think of saying. "Ai."

Just then Precious Grief let out a cackle that split the night like the backfire of a charcoal-burning truck. "Haw, haw, haw," he went. "Haw, haw, haw, haw, haw." He flapped from Chuck's shoulder to Pung's and tweeked Pung's ear fondly and painfully.

"We'll wake up all of Kunming," laughed Tien. "Come, let's go."

Quickly they returned to the custom-house gateway which

had given each of them its friendly shelter. Often in the future they would think of the place but now, in their joy at being reunited, it was nothing but an arch of yellow stone.

"How did you know we were here?" Tien asked as he buttoned his padded tunic and picked up Scarface's box.

"A man came and told us you might be at Chin Pi Lu so Pung and I came as fast as we could."

"Did he look like a smuggler?"

"A smuggler . . . ?" Tien tai-tai hesitated. "I don't know what he looked like. I hardly noticed. I just came as fast as I could."

Chuck suddenly thought of Scarface's present.

"Show Mother the box," he begged his father.

Tien pulled the draw. The light made the gold as pale as silver.

Tien tai-tai looked a little frightened at the sight of so much wealth.

"Where did you get it?"

Tien grinned. "From a friend," he said enigmatically. "Now let's get to our sampan. I want to be home."

Tien lifted Pung to his back. With Tien tai-tai on one side, and Chuck riding Precious Grief on his shoulder, they started across the bridge.

A flicker of light arcing into the water made Chuck turn. It was a cigarette burning brightly on its last flight. No careful Chinese ever flicked a cigarette like that, thought Chuck, and he stopped to rake the shadows with eager eyes. A man moved out from between two riverside houses. It was Captain Scott. He had returned to keep that last happy vigil with his friends.

Chuck waved.

The flyer waved back.

Chuck turned and followed his father and his mother and Pung.

The sun and the moon had parted. Would they ever meet again?